DRACHEN

DRACHEN

BRENDAN LE GRANGE

DRACHEN

ISBN 978-988-13617-0-7 (paperback)
ISBN 978-988-13617-1-4 (ebook)

© 2015 Brendan le Grange
http://BrendanleGrange.com
http://www.Twitter.com/BrendanleG

Edited and typeset by Alan Sargent
Cover design by Si Maclennan
Cover art © Si Maclennan 2015

For Bridget and Acacia

In Memory of Kevin Allen Moore

I

KALEV WAS running.

Roots grabbed his ankles. Leaves slapped his face. Branches picked threads from his jacket. He noticed none of it. He was focused, isolated from the insect calls that died and were resurrected by his coming and going. He was deep in a disorientating porcupine's back of silver birch trees, but that didn't slow him down either. He knew forests like this, he had grown up near one and become a killer in another.

To his left, a branch cracked under another running foot.

He adjusted his course, but he didn't ease up. On the contrary, this is what he lived for. It didn't matter that she was nimbler than him, that her small frame was less harassed in the narrow paths between the trees; he would catch his prey.

He barked a command to the two men behind him, eager for the woman to hear his words and know her approaching fate. The men shouted their acknowledgements as they spread to outflank her.

And Kalev kept running.

Brett was exhausted, running on adrenaline. She needed to stop, to rest, to breathe; just to stand still long enough to kill one of these damn mosquitoes would be a blessing. But the men were so close. She could hear their crass movements in the quiet moments between each beat of her heart. Their shouts, like the baying of wolves, chilled the humid night. And then there were the trees, which, like the men, seemed to be all around her, constricting her from all sides. She had to find a way through. She had to keep running.

Or stop.

For a moment, Brett thought of doing just that, of closing her eyes and giving up. But no, not when all she had to show for her work was a bag of trinkets and tangle of unanswered questions. She would run. She had given up on hope, though. Hope was for people running towards something and she was running away. She had fear and she was okay with that.

Brett burst into a small clearing illuminated by a cloud-shaded moon – twenty short seconds of unhindered progress – and then she re-entered the woods, risking a backwards glance just before she did: three torches blinked a warning, not far enough behind.

At least she had crested the hill and now the mulchy ground was sloping downwards. Towards the ferry pier? It didn't matter; she had to keep running.

Brett had been on the run for nearly five hours, and her body would give no more. She stumbled to her left, lurched forward then stopped, and then she heard it again. The soft and melodious gurgle of water. And suddenly she found more energy. A river would offer an unimpeded route down.

Brett shoved through the brambles that grew in a tight weave alongside the path, enduring their barbs but cursing the delay, until their resistance broke dramatically: she slid down a steep, muddy bank and into a shallow stream.

She cursed again, knelt for a quick drink and then pressed on. She was cold and wet and terrified, but the path in front of her was open. Soon she was even running again, her feet finding the river stones with more confidence than she had reason to expect.

Brett ran for twenty minutes like that, before she skidded to a stop. Ten metres ahead the stream began to growl and froth, and ten metres beyond that, in a thundering crescendo, it plunged over a cliff and out of sight. Her body froze. She didn't want it to, and she fought her rigid limbs, but only her head would move: it spun left and right and backwards, looking for another way. She focused her entire consciousness on her left foot, and moved it a step forward, then switched her attention to her right foot, begging it to follow.

Her heart worked itself into a frenzy.

No, she couldn't do it. She couldn't get any closer. The cliff would be too high. She just knew it would.

Kalev scanned the clearing. Spring in Finland meant a long twilight, which, complemented by the glow of his headlamp, revealed a scene in grey monochrome: a rectangular meadow, a hundred metres long and half as wide; two good sniper positions, both unmanned; knee-high grass shifting in the breeze, its pattern uniform and undisturbed except for a path recently stamped through its centre. He tracked the path's trajectory to where the forest started again. There was movement there. Or was there? It was too fleeting for him to confirm. Forests like this were full of life, large and small, natural and maybe even supernatural. He smiled to himself; perhaps he'd seen a Hiisi, a troll from one of his grandmother's stories. It didn't matter. If there was a Hiisi out there tonight, he'd catch it too. But he was certain he had seen his prey. They were very close. He hyperventilated with a dozen quick breaths, followed by a single extended exhale, and resumed the chase.

The clearing ended abruptly, damning his lanky frame to a renewed battering from the low branches and ratcheting him down to half pace.

Kalev's enforced go-slow had its benefits, however, when two broken branches snagged in his peripheral vision. Someone had left the path, heading urgently eastwards, straight through the natural barricades. Kalev followed, for who would struggle through the undergrowth rather than go around it, except someone running for her life?

His prey was panicking and he was enjoying it.

Her path cut through a thicket of brambles and ended at the scarred, muddy bank of a shallow stream. She had entered it there, and he could see no signs of her getting out. Clever. But streams are like railway tracks: the route they provide is smoother, but also more predictable.

Kalev slid down the bank. Waited. Listened. And sprinted forward. Then the world exploded into white.

2

KALEV DROPPED to his knees. Everything was still white. But he didn't need visual cues to find and cock his gun. He fired a covering burst of three shots.

Nothing in response. A mistake, she would never get such an easy chance again.

He massaged his eyes against the pain; the random and transient patterns that it brought to life were at least a sign that his vision was returning. He fired another burst of three as a balm for his anger.

It was the second time that day that she'd used the boat's flare gun in her escape. And it was the second time that day he'd fallen for it. He was losing his edge.

Kalev fired two more shots in frustration, ejected the spent magazine, smashed home a fresh one, blinked to make sure his vision was stable, and started to climb down the damp side of the waterfall. She was somewhere down there.

His two companions would know to follow.

In hindsight, it had been a stroke of genius: although the delay switch she'd cobbled together had probably been much more likely to fail than to succeed, so perhaps luck should be given some of the credit. It was the hunters' crude chants, the same ones that had haunted her escape, that had broken the waterfall's spell. Her legs moved when she heard them approaching, turning her away from the waterfall's terrible height, and powering her up the stream's bank.

Hiding behind a fallen tree, she watched the hunters get closer. She had to improvise: she jammed a stone behind the flare gun's trigger; looped her hair band around it to hold it tight. Now all she could do was hope that when she tossed the rigged flare gun over the waterfall, the impact of its landing would knock the stone loose and allow the elastic to squeeze the trigger and fire the flare.

The men were very close.

And then they were standing at the waterfall, looking down.

She had wanted the burning flare to lure them onwards, to create an opportunity for her to slip their net before they noticed the marked stream bank, but the Fates had smiled on her. Instead of shooting upwards like a call for help, the flare had flown directly at the tallest of the men, forcing him to drop to his knees to avoid being singed. And that had pissed him off.

Now he and his henchmen were chasing phantoms and she was escaping.

It was an hour before Brett felt safe enough to slow to a walk, which is why the first shot came as such a surprise.

Brett dodged behind a tree. Two more shots whistled past and she was running again. With her head hunched, she sprinted forward as a bullet cut through a sapling inches to her right, close enough to send her stumbling to the ground.

More shots flew over her head.

Kalev was in a foul mood; a mood that catching up with his prey had done little to improve. He'd had to terminate the employment of his two hired guns, but that wasn't why he was upset. They had seen him make too many mistakes. He knew that and they knew that, albeit too late. The fact was, though, he had made mistakes, plural, and that had to stop.

His first shots had been to flush her out, and it had worked. Now, as he leaned against a tree, he took aim more carefully and fired five times in quick succession.

She went down.

Kalev lowered his weapon and charged after her, immediately making another mistake. It couldn't have been a good hit, because she was up again and heading for thicker cover. He emptied the clip with hurried shots that threatened nothing except the foliage.

3

B RETT COMBED her hands through her shoulder-length
mahogany hair, dragging out a nest of twigs and leaves;
she had tried to clean her hardwearing cargo shorts in the boat's
small bathroom, but while they were less obviously muddy,
there was no hiding the fact that they were torn; her jacket had
been lost and her T-shirt holed front and back during her
escape. She looked a mess. Still, she felt fantastic and the sight
of land promised an end to her epic journey. She stretched.
Okay, maybe 'fantastic' wasn't the right word; her body ached
too much for that, but she certainly felt relieved.

Brett had assumed that the men who were chasing her had
seen her board the ferry and would have arranged to have
someone waiting when it docked at Röölä. So instead of
walking into a trap, she had stowed away for the ferry's return
trip.

After two hours spent lying like coiled rope on the planks
of a covered lifeboat, she had enjoyed just ten comfortable
minutes on dry land before boarding a different ferry to the
neighbouring island of Pakinainen, where she had inserted
herself into a tour group on the back end of its island-hopping
daytrip.

Now, as she scanned the approaching harbour for threats, her plan seemed to have worked. Seemed to. She couldn't be sure, so she kept watching.

Brett's adopted companions disembarked and headed to a waiting bus and since no one stopped her, she followed them aboard to Helsinki and, as soon as she could, out of Finland.

She wasn't going to let the trail go cold.

Brett rushed through a shower and dressed in a pair of fitted jeans, a white button-down blouse, and hand-stitched calfskin boots – all made in Milan and bought the day before in one of Tallinn's monumental new shopping malls.

It was the last thing she'd managed to do before dropping into bed and sleeping for fourteen hours straight. And now she was almost late for her appointment, over-dressed for the neighbourhood, but feeling almost normal again. She was standing in front of a prop from a cheap horror movie. Green paint curled from the wooden cladding of a house that swayed visibly in the gusting wind. But it was in no way beneath its peers. In fact, the dented Lada parked out front gave it an air of relative prosperity. Tallinn's forty-five years of Communist rule was not best illustrated by the tourist gem of the Old Town or the glass fronted skyscrapers rising beside it, but by neighbourhoods like this. She rapped on the door and waited.

This was her last chance. The man she was there to meet had been described to her as 'strange', apparently well known in the *Drachen* community for his hermetic lifestyle and his persistent claim that an ancestor of his late wife had been a crewman aboard the ship. That she was standing on his doorstep now was testament to how slim her options were.

Creaking floorboards extended the foreboding before a weary face peered out. 'Bretta?'

She nodded. 'Call me Brett, please.'

The old man looked left and right, and then ushered her in. 'I'm Rasmus, please come inside. Please, through there, take a seat.' He waved her towards a fraying lounge: striped wallpaper, a dangling lightbulb behind a burnt shade, an overflowing bookshelf and some of its surplus volumes stacked as sidetables beside two mottled armchairs that were turned towards each other. One of those chairs bore his imprint in its sunken springs, so Brett sat in the other. 'I was just making coffee, would you fancy a cup?'

'Yes, please.'

While Brett waited for Rasmus to return, she beat some dust out of the armrests and straightened the closest stack of books; her thoughts were already a mess, she couldn't handle more chaos in the furnishings. Could this man really help? Probably not. The adrenaline was out of her system now and filling its place was a rising sense of realism, she'd almost certainly missed her chance when the dive site was hijacked. In fact, she probably never had a chance. But she had found the wreck, so anything was possible.

Rasmus handed Brett a fresh cup of steaming Arabica and took his seat without the creaks or complaints of most men his age, picking up the envelope she'd left on his chair as he did so. 'You've come about the book, you said.'

'Well, more than that, now. I've actually come to ask about the ship.'

Rasmus wedged the envelope between the cushion and the armrest and leaned forward. Brett had such vivid eyes, unexpectedly blue amidst olive-toned Mediterranean features. 'Do you mean. . . .' He swallowed, made to start again, and then left the question unfinished.

'I do,' she said, answering anyway. Rasmus sat up straighter. 'I found the *Drachen,* in remarkably good condition actually, lying on her port side about sixty metres down, between Turku and the Åland Islands.' Brett stopped and Rasmus jumped in. 'How?'

'Three years of research and, in the end, some luck. Basically, I found a painting that showed the sinking of the *Drachen.* Using the shape of the islands in the background, and the recorded histories of the two Swedish-flagged warships I could identify, I was able to narrow the location of the battle to a searchable region. Took me two weeks to locate it and cut my way inside.'

'Finland. Very Interesting. A bit off track . . . that is why it was never found before, I suppose. No, it could make sense, I guess. They could have been sailing to Visby.' Rasmus had picked up his coffee, though he made no move to drink it. 'But tell me, what was it like?'

'It was beautiful.' Brett paused, cracked her knuckles, and shook off her reverie. 'Well, not aesthetically beautiful, its design is purely functional, but beautiful, just, beautiful. Jesus, it nearly got me killed – but it was beautiful.'

'Killed? What? What happened?'

'I was hijacked. Some thugs raided my dive boat the day I got inside. The lazy buggers were probably waiting for that.'

'What? Are you okay?'

Brett waved away his concern. 'I was betrayed but, hey, what can you expect? Men are easily corruptible and I spoke too freely about my goal. Look, perhaps it would have hurt more if it had mattered. As it happens, it made no real difference.'

'What do you mean?'

Even Brett's forced smile vanished as she slumped back against the creaking backrest. 'Just what I said, none of it mattered, the whole exercise was pointless. The *Drachen* was guarded by loyal skeletons and rusted cannons but the cupboard was bare, so to speak. There was no treasure.'

'But did you find anything?'

'What? Were you even listening? No. Nothing. That's why I'm here. I was told that you were a man who could help but I'm not so sure anymore. It's not your fault, really, it is what it is. You can keep your fee, but I think I'm wasting my time. Sorry, I think I should just go home now.'

Brett began to cry. And Rasmus let her for a minute. 'Brett, let's talk. I think I can help, and if it turns out I can't, then you can keep your money; that's not what I'm after. First, though, you need to tell me if you found anything down there. Anything at all.'

'Nothing. I found nothing. The hold had already been looted. There was no gold, there were no jewels, just four cannons and the giant hole they'd blasted in the hull to scuttle her; only a few trinkets from the captain's private quarters.' Brett lifted an olive Barbour duffle bag onto her lap. Though she'd bought it new it was all waxed cotton twill and leather straps, so it looked even better with the nicks and scratches it had since acquired – very vintage. After a quick search, she pulled out a neoprene dive bag and emptied its contents onto the floor: six gold coins, pitted with age and exposure, clattered on the wood, followed by a thumping sphere of hazy amber the size of a grapefruit, and a set of ancient keys.

Rasmus released a breath he'd been holding since her fingers first touched the bag's ties. 'And you have the book.' He pointed to the book she cradled on her lap, its cover aged to the colour of fertile earth and branded in the top right corner with a single, airborne dragon.

'Yes, I've always had the book, but it was a painting that solved the mystery.'

Rasmus shook his head. 'Tell me how much you know about the *Drachen*.'

Brett stared back at him silently.

'Please.'

'Which version do you want to hear, the realistic or the fanciful?

'Both.' He was grinning as he settled into his chair. He sipped his coffee and waved for her to continue.

'Well, the *Drachen* was a warship built by the Hanseatic League in the late fourteenth century, the biggest and fastest on the seas, not surpassed for eighty years. It was also something of a naval folly and a resource drain; turns out they would have done better to focus on building more of their existing warships because, despite its individual prowess, it succumbed to overwhelming enemy numbers and was lost in some forgotten skirmish without ever achieving its potential. At least that's the version that won't get you laughed out of town. Then there is the romantic version,' she said, tapping the book, 'that says the *Drachen* was commissioned to retrieve some grand treasure and that, having found the treasure and tamed the dragon that once guarded it, they took the dragon aboard as their talisman and went on to battle fantastic beasts and foreign armies as they sailed home.'

'And which version do you believe?'

'Obviously the former. And I found the *Drachen* by linking it to a painting of a sea battle, so I guess that proves it. Though as I said, it appeared scuttled rather than sunk, probably to avoid capture.'

'And the wreck you found was the wreck of a fighting craft, yes?'

'Well. Okay, no. It was designed more like a floating safe than a fighting machine, but. . . .'

'But what if the truth lies somewhere in the middle of your two versions? What if only the fantastical beasts were fiction, not the *Drachen*'s treasure-gathering purpose? What if the *Drachen*'s history was intentionally unbelievable? I don't think you found nothing, Brett, I think you found everything.'

She was looking straight at him now. 'What are you talking about?'

'The *Drachen* was designed as a conventional warship, but its construction was expedited and its mission redefined in 1387 when the Hanseatic League learned of a quite extraordinary treasure.'

Brett nodded.

'Let me start by going back a little further in time, to tell you about Jaume Ferrer. He was a Majorcan explorer who left Europe in 1346, heading for West Africa and the fabled River of Gold. Other than a mention in the *Catalan Atlas,* which placed him near the Canary Islands shortly thereafter, he was never seen again and was presumed lost at sea. The Hansa, however, learned of another story.'

'That he had in fact found this River of Gold?'

'No, Jaume had abandoned that search early – when he learned of a much, much more magnificent treasure.'

'And the Hansa learned that he had found it?'

'No. Jaume died in Africa without ever finding any gold, but he had a son. . . .'

How did people manage to live up here? Jaime Ferrer squinted into the heat haze that seemed to stretch in every direction, and shook his head. Two days ago they had climbed out of the forests and entered the mangy highlands and they hadn't passed a source of fresh water since. Some of the horses had died, some of the men weren't far behind, and they were all starting to get restless.

They were close, though. He'd been watching for the clues in the bare landscape: the shape of the ridge; the scar of an ancient riverbed; even the route the shadows took as the sun set. Everything was as his father had calculated. Jaime dropped onto his haunches and tested the burning sand through his fingers, lifted a pinch to his tongue. Exactly as his father had calculated.

'Dig here,' he ordered, before grabbing a shovel himself.

They had found the entrance to the canyons, 500 leagues of interconnecting and deadending veins that ran deep below the desert. This was not their end goal. The canyons' cool confines would be just as treacherous as the white-hot expanse above. Indeed, they had been a bridge too far for his father. But they were an important step, because Jaime Ferrer had an advantage his father never did.

Born of the union between the great explorer and the daughter of a local chief, Jaime had grown up in the royal household. Still, it had taken him thirty-four years to overhear enough court gossip to finish the map, thirty-four years in which he'd watched his father grow sick and die. Now those years were about to bear fruit.

He summoned his strongest men and set off. It didn't matter that the path was dark and that their torches were asthmatic underground; he knew he'd smell the treasure before he saw it.

4

'WHAT DID he find?' Brett was interested now.
'I don't know.'

Rasmus laughed and Brett felt heat rising in her cheeks; this was going nowhere, he was just another crackpot. 'You don't know?'

'No, the treasure was never described. But his father was heading to Africa under royal decree and so to abandon his duties to search for this treasure was also to sentence himself to death and his family to a life of poverty and servitude unless he struck it rich. Since he took up the search – and since his son continued it – we have to assume that they believed that it justified that risk. And at that time, the ancient kingdom of Mali, where I believe he landed, was famed for its wealth in gold. It was once home to Mansa Musa, the richest man the world has ever known, so nothing is out of the question.'

'Okay, let's assume it's gold then, a lot of gold. If Jaime found it, why didn't he just send a messenger to Majorca requesting an escort home?'

'It was thirty years since his dad had disappeared. No one in Majorca even knew Jaume had a son, and if they did, well, they were not above condemning a son for the sins of his father. For

Jaime to get the king to believe his story – and thus perhaps to forgive his father's dereliction of duty – he would have to arrive with proof. So that's what he set out to do. He shanghaied a crew of natives, loaded his father's patched-up galley with as much of the treasure as it could carry, and set course for Majorca.'

'So the Hansa sent the *Drachen* to West Africa to intercept him?'

'The *Drachen* was sent to intercept the young Ferrer's galley as it neared the Mediterranean; and to bring the stolen treasure to Germany. Hence the name by the way, *Drachen* being the German for "dragon", the protectors of treasure. Anyway, neither the younger Ferrer nor the *Drachen* was ever heard from again, until you found proof that the *Drachen* did make it home.'

'So the treasure has to be real, too?'

'I've always thought so.'

'Okay, so then it was stolen. Like I said, the hold was empty so it doesn't matter.'

'But since you found the wreck off the coast of Finland, there's reason to believe the other stories, too.'

'I don't understand. Are you saying that you believe that the crew fought sea monsters, ghost ships, and dragons?'

'Not exactly. The *Drachen* succeeded; the treasure was captured at sea and brought to Germany, ending the story as far as Jaime Ferrer is concerned. And then the treasure was hidden again, which is where your book comes in.'

'I don't understand.'

'The treasure wasn't on the *Drachen* when it sunk, but clues to its hiding place might have been. When the treasure first arrived in Lübeck, it made quite a stir and divided the leadership of the League. Some saw it as a windfall to be used immediately. Others saw it as a war chest to be saved for a rainy day: with tensions already discernible along their borders, those men realised that there would come a time when the League had the need for it, and they felt it would be foolish to act before then. It was the latter group that prevailed. They hid the treasure and sent the *Drachen* to scatter clues to its location across the Hanseatic world. The wreck you found is testament to at least the partial success of that second mission.'

'Okay then, in which cities did they hide those clues? Because if you haven't been paying attention, I found none aboard the *Drachen.*'

Rasmus grinned again and rubbed his hands together. 'I don't know. Fearing the seeds of dissent they'd already seen would take root and crack the Hansa into factions, those few elders acted alone, and they took their secrets with them to their graves. I don't even know how many clues there were, but I'm sure this amber sphere is one of them.'

Brett rolled the hazy sphere in her hand, 'How is *this* a clue?'
'I don't know.'

'Of course. And the coins?' She felt a headache coming on.

'No, those are just old coins, though you're sure to get a decent price for them from the right collector. It's the sphere that we're after. The legend says that the captain's log book . . .' He looked again at the book she held '. . . holds the code; that a key will unlock the code to reveal a dragon, and that the dragon will lead you to the treasure's final hiding place.'

Brett eyed the dusty amber. 'This will lead us to the treasure?'

'It has to. That's why I want to hear about anything else on board. If this sphere was the only one, then it stands to reason that it was destined to be the final clue and so, assuming the trail ran backwards towards the treasure, it gives us a place to start.'

'How do you know all of this?'

'How do you know whether to trust me, you mean?' He was still grinning, but a quaver in his voice betrayed his emotion.

'You're right to question my credentials and I'll be honest and say that I can't be sure of any of this. Since my Karyn died, I've searched even harder, for her, piecing together rumours and third-hand accounts, but still I can prove nothing. I have always believed it, though. Now, since you've found the wreck, I'm willing to believe it even more.'

Brett sipped her cold coffee, and weighed up her options. She did need a push, but in which direction was this man going to send her?

5

B RETT WAS sitting on the floor with the old book open in front of her. Its scratched leather cover protected vellum pages of exquisite beauty: the page Brett had it open on carried a woodcut illustration of medieval Tallinn across one whole page, facing a calligraphed story whose initial letter was illuminated with gold leaf.

When she told Rasmus that she'd always had the book, she had been fibbing; the book had come into her possession six years ago, a surreptitious acquisition from the archives of the University of Hamburg. Brett had been a visiting professor there for two semesters and found the book neglected, unwatched, and irresistible. A week later the university had received an anonymous endowment to even the scales.

'It's beautiful.' Rasmus had come back into the room, carrying two cups of fresh coffee. 'And so is this, now.' He placed the amber globe on the floor next to Brett. Polished, it looked like a tiny full moon, and it gave off a charming forest scent. Brett's eyes dove deeper. A delicate golden dragon, so well carved that it could still be alive, flew through liquid light. 'So, what do you make of it?' he asked.

'Isn't that what I'm paying you for?'

'Well, it's one of the dragons, of course. I know that it's meaningful, I just don't know *what* it means!' He smiled at his own wordplay. Brett fidgeted, she wasn't sure how much more of his non-answers she could handle. 'Amber is an interesting substance: it's resin, not a mineral, of course, flammable and mildly magnetic. It was valued by the Hansa and they were skilled in its use, so I'm not surprised to see it.'

Brett tapped the page. 'Now it's my turn to play professor. How much do you know about the book?'

Rasmus was standing very close, his hands inching forward and jerking back continuously, leaning so far forward that she barely had room to turn the pages.

'I have read that the captain's message was spun into a collection of fairy tales, is that true?'

'Maybe ... for example, take this story. The citizens of Tallinn had kept an uneasy peace with a dragon that lived in a cave in Toompea Rock: for as long as they delivered it a regular supply of sacrificial pigs and sheep, it left them alone.

'One autumn, a fierce storm blew off the Baltic, forcing the *Drachen* to seek cover in Tallinn's harbour and subjugating the land to nineteen days of gale force winds and torrential rain. Crops were uprooted; fields were waterlogged; coops, pens, and stables were flattened. It would be a long winter. Nevertheless, fearing the wrath of a hungry dragon, the mayor sent their standard tribute. Many had objected, of course, but in the end he won out.

'So the whole town rejoiced when the fifteen men who had gone to deliver the twenty-three sheep and fifty-five chickens returned no less burdened. They had found the dragon's lair flooded and the dragon dead. The mayor even decreed a feast day in honour of their liberation.

'However, one little girl had liked the dragon and didn't want to believe it was dead. So, while the rest of the town feasted, she snuck away from her home, hiked through the fields, and climbed the slick rock face to reach the flooded lair.

'She couldn't help herself, she screamed when she saw movement. It wasn't the dragon, though. The dragon was dead. It was an egg. And it was rocking back and forth on the uneven floor as she watched. Then the egg began to crack.

'She couldn't leave a baby dragon there, alone, so she cradled it back to Tallinn; but she knew that the people would kill it if they found out, so she went to the one man in town who might help.

'And indeed, the captain of the *Drachen* knew the value of a custodial dragon, for the small cost of a few pigs and goats Tallinn had thrived for thirty-five peaceful years, unmolested by its neighbours. He also knew how he could help. He took the little girl and her hatchling to a church where a trustworthy abbot owed him a favour. The abbot offered the dragon refuge in the cellar and the girl a place in the attached school. Over time, the bond between the two grew stronger, while outside the town's memories faded. Until Tallinn came under attack.

'A massive force of Danish raiders were at the gates. Greater in number and better armed than the defenders, they were on the brink of breaching the city's gates when the dragon emerged, unbidden. The Danes dropped their weapons and fled, never to return.'

'What do you think it means?' Rasmus asked.

She shrugged. 'Other than sounding like the propaganda of a military dictator, it just sounds like a story to me. You said that the book holds the code, though, so could it be an obtuse way of telling us that the clue is hidden in a church?'

'Churches are among the few buildings from those days that might still be standing today.'

'So, which church?'

6

THE LAST two weeks had taken their toll on Hiko. His eyes were dry and red, his hair was growing out – any longer and it would start to curl – and his stomach hadn't settled since arriving in Hong Kong. He rolled over. And over again. He couldn't sleep. Not the way he felt now. Not in such a restricted space. As the son of a Vietnamese mother and Japanese father, he was never going to be tall, and yet here he was in a room where he could touch all four walls simultaneously. And that room leaked. And it rocked. He hated that constant rocking. In fact, the room possessed only one redeeming factor: it wasn't in Paris.

Not that there is anything wrong with Paris. It might be over-priced, and dirty, and its citizens might be rude to tourists, but none of that bothered Hiko. In truth, he had quite enjoyed living there. For a while. He had become concerned, however, with the level of policing. In particular, he had become concerned with the level of policing actively engaged in looking for him. He checked his phone. There was still no call from Finland. And that was another problem with the room: the reception was appalling.

He rolled over again, but he knew that he wouldn't fall back to sleep, not until he'd heard from Kalev, anyway.

Kalev's team had captured the dive site easily. They'd even sent back pictures from the wreck. But then they'd let the woman get away and now there was a growing chance of Hiko's plan unravelling before it was implemented.

He wouldn't let his mother be that lucky. He fumed at the thought. His mother. He hadn't seen her in six years. Not since he punched her and left.

That made it sound worse than it was: hitting a woman, and his own mother to boot. But it was only one punch. And she had been warned. When Hiko was ten years old. It hadn't stayed her hand that day, but she hadn't forgotten either. He knew, because he'd stared into her eyes during every beating he'd endured from that day forward and had seen it there, that memory. No, she hadn't forgotten, she had just thought he was too weak to follow through. God knows he had given her reason to doubt. He had probably been big enough to strike back when he was thirteen. He had definitely been big enough when he was fifteen. And yet he didn't act until nearly three years later. Not because he was unsure. No, definitely not. He knew exactly what he wanted: more justice than simple battery could deliver.

Hiko had also wanted the money his parents had stolen from the bank. Now he had it and he was spending it well. At least it had looked that way, until Kalev started screwing up.

Hiko got out of bed, made himself a strong cup of bad coffee, and took it to the upper deck. The rising sun was painting his neighbours in pastel shades: three dozen fishing boats, with their cluttered decks and tattered plastic coverings, seesawed on the oily surface between a similar number of larger trawlers and past-their-prime working craft.

His temporary base was an old fireboat. An almost even mix of rust and faded red paint decorated its hull, showing its age to the outside world as authoritatively as its dripping pipes and creaking frame did to him on board. At some point someone had tried to spruce it up: overlapping stripes of military grey paint had been applied to the superstructure, though whoever had done that had lost heart before the job was completed.

If there was one thing about the fireboat that could be considered beautiful, it would be the water cannons that characterised its silhouette: two facing forward and one facing back. His landlord – as much as that term could be applied, given the pedantic lack of land and the old man's dubious claim of legal ownership – had promised that they were functional, yet the shower produced more noise than water. Nevertheless, they were what had sealed the deal.

Of course the anonymity of the location was important, too. The fireboat was anchored in the Shau Kei Wan Typhoon Shelter, a time capsule of a suburb on the eastern outskirts of Hong Kong Island, where the lava of urban gentrification finally cools to a stop. Here the local boat people kept to themselves; the last lonely survivors of Hong Kong's modernisation, they had as much to lose by interacting with outsiders as Hiko did.

He sipped his coffee and spun his phone on the table. That call still hadn't come. He couldn't wait. He picked up the phone and dialled.

'You have her.'

'We don't, not yet.'

'Not yet. Kalev, I am not an unreasonable man. If this is beyond your abilities, I am willing to annul our contract. Simply return the funds you have already received by tomorrow afternoon, and I'll let you walk away. Of course, you'll have to cover the costs already incurred, but. . . .'

'No, sir, it's under control. We're getting close.'

'Close is not going to suffice for much longer, Kalev.'

'Yes, sir.'

7

B RETT STILL had the book open in front of her, and now it was flanked by a tourist map of Tallinn's Old Town, with all of the churches highlighted in luminous yellow. There weren't as many as she had feared. Nevertheless, searching every one of them would take too long, so she needed a way to cull the list of candidates. That meant rereading the book and assuming everything was a clue. She started to make a list.

'Fifteen men is a strange number to carry twenty-three sheep, don't you think?' Brett didn't look up as she spoke.

'What do you mean?'

Brett laughed, finally it was her turn to baffle Rasmus with a cryptic question. 'Don't you think it's strange that the story has such specific numbers in it, or am I reading too much into this?'

'Well, numbers would certainly be a good way to encode data; but they didn't use survey coordinates, did they?'

They didn't have street numbers back then, either, and they didn't look like dates. Unless they mashed the fifteen and the thirty-seven together, that was a reasonable date for a church to have been built, as was the fifteen and almost any one of the other numbers, though. That was the problem; it felt too arbitrary, especially since none of the dates they constructed uniquely identified any of the major churches in town.

The most basic code would match each number to a letter, perhaps rolling through the alphabet for larger numbers, so that one and twenty-seven both meant 'A'. But if there was a six-letter word that identified a particular church, was it written in Estonian? Or German? Or scrambled? She only came up with 'sowiac', which seemed unlikely to work in any tongue.

Basically, nothing worked unless she forced it to, and even then it didn't really work.

'Wait, look here.' Brett flipped to the fifteenth page, then to the nineteenth, then to the twenty-third. 'If the numbers refer to specific pages, then every page mentioned is the start of a story.'

'That has to be significant.'

'If it has to be significant, and I agree with you that it has to be, then it can only be because of this.' Brett tapped the top of the page. The first letter of every story was decorated, but in a non-traditional way: embossed in gold leaf, the letters stood bold above backgrounds of loosely-wrapped ribbons in red, blue, yellow, and white. 'It's these ribbons, look at the ribbons.'

Rasmus pushed his glasses snug against the bridge of his nose and stared at the jumble of colour. 'Do you think the colours are symbolic of something? I've never heard anything about that before.'

Brett flipped through the pages again, though slower now, and stopped each time she reached the beginning of a new tale. 'No, it's simpler than that.' She turned back to the fifty-fifth page. 'See, remember this . . .' She tapped the pattern of red, yellow, and blue ribbons, and then turned to the thirty-fifth page, '. . . and this . . .' she flipped to the twenty-third page, '. . . and this. Every one of the pages mentioned includes a red ribbon.'

'I see. And I assume that's important.' Rasmus wasn't looking nearly as excited as she was feeling.

'Yes. Yes. Very definitely, yes. Red ribbons occur on other pages too, but sporadically, and then there's this: do you see how if we were to place page twenty-three alongside page five their red ribbons would line up perfectly?'

'Where are you going with this?'

Brett scrambled across the room to fetch her iPad. She scanned in each of the images and shuffled them around, turning some over, turning some of them back, until the six illuminated letters created a grid two wide and three high: the red ribbons intersecting seamlessly down the middle to form something that could pass as a map. Albeit a basic one. And if it was a map, the small gold cross in the top right sextant was its only notable feature.

Brett handed Rasmus the screen. 'Please tell me you recognise this place? Just look at the red lines.'

'Brett, please, a few rough lines? It could be anywhere, or nowhere.'

While Brett was earning her PhD, she had volunteered in one of Napoli's toughest neighbourhoods, offering free mathematics lessons to elementary school pupils for extra teaching credit – if there was one thing that taught you, it was how to give an effective death stare. Brett hit Rasmus with her best.

'Okay, okay, I'll try.' Rasmus made a rectangle with his index fingers and thumbs, then tracked it over the tourist map, looking back and forth between the two images. 'Here. Here!

It's the old town, from the Town Hall in the north, I'd say, to the Kiek in de Kok tower in the south.'

'And the cross, where is that?'

'Well, that would be the Town Hall. It's not a church, but it is famous for its dragon-design rainspouts. And it would have been around at the right time. You've done it!'

Long green necks and gold-crowned dragon heads looked down onto Town Hall Square from a roof too high for the building's single line of windows. Brett and Rasmus moved carefully through a gothic arcade, before entering a series of cramped rooms decorated with mannequins in period costume. There wasn't much for them there, just blank stone floors and whitewashed walls.

They climbed to the main level and dared to hope. Here, the interior resembled a church with its vaulted ceilings, herringbone pillars, and rows of straight-backed public seating. Intricate tapestries decorated the white walls. Brett's hope waned, though, as she grasped the scope of the search.

A fruitless two hours later, having exhausted their options, they moved upstairs to the cosier parlour. Plush wallpaper and warm lighting did nothing to hide the fact that it, too, was bare of clues.

'What do you think?'

Rasmus flattened the wrinkles in his right cheek, then brought his hand under his chin in thought. 'We've missed something.'

'You're kidding? We didn't miss anything, there's nothing here to find.'

'That's not what I meant. I think we've missed something in the clue.' He checked his watch. 'Let's go and have lunch and see if we can spot what it was.'

Brett hoped he was right; the alternative was a very sudden dead end.

'It always felt wrong, didn't it?' Rasmus asked. They were sitting in a cellar-level restaurant across the square, warming themselves with coffees fortified by a shot of Grand Marnier. 'It not being a church, I mean.'

Brett nodded but didn't say anything; she was thinking about what he had said earlier. *The right key will unlock the code and the code will unlock the treasure's final hiding place.* Maps all had a key, but ... *'The right key.'*

'What?'

'The right key. The keys. It's literal. It has something to do with the keys.' Brett scratched in her bag and withdrew the ancient keys. She flicked through them. There were seven in total, each identical in size, each made out of the same tarnished bronze, and each declaring its purpose with glaring clarity, now that she really looked at them: instead of a row of turret shaped teeth, these keys all ended in a single square tooth punctured by a stylised cross, one that matched the cross on the map exactly. 'What if the gold cross is not a marker for the end goal, but a marker for the starting point?'

Brett positioned the key so that its cut-out aligned with the gold cross on the map. She pointed to the location now circled by the key's oval bow. 'Please tell me there is a church right over there.'

Rasmus moved the drinks and spread the tourist map across the table, exploring it with a shaking fingertip. 'I'm sorry, there's nothing significant there.'

'There has to be. Ah, damn. It's because of this.' The keys were all the same, except each cross was offset at a different angle. Because of this unique offset, while each key could align perfectly with the cross on the map, it indicated a different part of town when it did so. Brett studied the key in her hand, turned it over, held it up to the light. The key's shank was marked. She blinked. Or were those innocent scratches?

No, they were intentional. A tiny dragon had been carved three quarters of the way down. It was too small to say for sure, but it looked a lot like the dragon within the amber, except its wings were now at rest. Brett grabbed another key. It had a dragon marking, too, again, almost the same as the one in the amber. She smiled.

This one had to be the right key. It was an ingenious safety device, too: each found dragon indicated the next key to use, so that only someone who had the previous clue could find the next one. Brett placed the key on the map and looked at Rasmus. 'So?'

Rasmus referred to the tourist map again. 'St Nicholas Church. And it ticks all the boxes.' He pushed his chair back and picked up his bag. 'What are you waiting for? We can eat on the way.'

The tower of St Nicholas' Church was a prominent feature of Tallinn's skyline; its black and green Baroque spire might not have been as tall as that of St Olaf's, but it had more character. It was also one of the oldest churches in Tallinn, having been built by German and Swedish merchants in 1275. And since it

41

predated the building of the city walls, it had been fortified its whole life and resembled a citadel as much as it did a place of worship. They arrived as the last tour group of the day was filing in.

Feigning interest in the Spanish-speaking guide's excited monologue, they walked in and, as the tourists receded towards Bernt Notke's famous Danse Macabre painting, got to work.

An hour later, and harassed by the caretaker's vociferous reminders about the closing time, they met back at the door. The church's plastered walls and recesses were sparingly decorated with muted sculptures, gilt-framed paintings, and not a single marker left by the crew of the *Drachen*.

Another dead end.

8

MATTHYS ROSSOUW put down the phone. He pushed his chair back, raised his head, made sure none of his colleagues were within earshot, and swore loudly (though he probably didn't need to bother with such social niceties, considering he always swore in his native Flemish). Since taking the position at Europol, he spoke almost exclusively in English – he had even started to dream in his adoptive language – but there were some sentiments that could only be properly expressed in his guttural mother tongue: the man he was after had vanished.

St George. A name he had come up with when he first linked three open case files to a hypothetical single perpetrator, one obsessed with all types of dragon iconography.

His nickname hadn't stuck.

Nor, indeed, had his single-perpetrator theory. The French, the Germans, and the Danes, they had all refused to see reason, each continuing to pursue their own unique phantom independently, and often at odds with one another. 'Art thieves always specialise in a period, sometimes in a single artist. Never in a theme.' They had not so much said that last line as chuckled it.

And they had managed to convince his boss, a too-sensible Frenchwoman, of the same. She had expressly told him not to spend any more time on the case – and that had been a week ago, when there were still fresh reports coming out of the Paris underworld. Now, even those sources had run dry. Obviously he hadn't stopped, though.

Matthys ran a hand through his prematurely thinning hair. *Verdamme,* he was only thirty. He needed a coffee. He looked at his list of unread email. Actually, he needed something stronger than a coffee, but a coffee would have to do. And then he'd have to start doing his real work. Though it seemed an ethereal focus for the efforts of Europe's leading police force, did the people really need to be protected from fake Jimmy Choo handbags? Was that going to be the defining blow in the battle for the future of his unborn children?

Unlikely.

He would write his report, though; and on time, he owed his boss that much. It would mean staying late that evening, breaking a date, and thus further delaying the hypothetical conception of his unborn children, he noted self-pityingly, but it would also free up time on Friday afternoon to chase down a lead.

He was the wrong type to hold down a responsible career.

9

BRETT'S MOOD improved as she walked back through the charming old town. Tallinn felt extra special at twilight; weather vanes turned briefly gold and reflected pink clouds in the puddles that seemed to form between cobblestones even when it hadn't been raining; only a dusting of snow could have dressed it up better. The walk back to her hotel took her past the Blackheads' House, with its spectacular green, red, and gold door closed to the public at that hour, through the grounds of the illuminated Fat Margret Tower, with its squat round body and cut-off conical roof that was so much a part of the old town's look and feel, and then out of the dream, across a busy road, and into the ferry terminal. Tallinn was beautiful, her hotel was not.

She had checked into the ferry company's own budget accommodation, a property that strived to meet the simple needs of the Finnish tourists who made the two hour trip from Helsinki to stock up on duty-free liquor. The bed was passable, but the walls were paper thin and she could hear each beer being opened as a party vibrated to life in the room next door.

It would be a long night.

Brett prepared a space on the desk. Knowing she wouldn't get to sleep any time soon, Brett started to research Tallinn and its churches. She was starting from square one again, but maybe there was another way to crack this egg.

Four hours later, she was bogged down in a fug. Like a weary driver on a long straight road, she was too tired to function but too hyped up to sleep. She was being nagged by the conviction that she already had everything she needed to solve the puzzle.

Brett jerked awake at 2 AM. She had fallen asleep in the desk chair, so the map was right in front of her. St Nicholas was the obvious choice. And it would have been the obvious choice then. Even more so. Too obvious.

With just the book, someone could have put together the map and its golden cross over Town Hall. She knew that was decoy number one. With the map and the key, they could have gone one step further and identified St Nicholas Church. Had the clue that had once been hidden there been lost in one of the many wars or restorations, or was that decoy number two? An inbuilt failsafe in case a conspirator was ever captured; a way for them to appease their captors without actually compromising the treasure, perhaps. If so, what else could she use?

There weren't many other options. Brett picked up the key. There weren't any other options, actually.

Brett turned the key in her hand. Instead of laying the key across the map from its top right corner down towards its centre, she turned it so that it ran diagonally upwards and into the white space beyond its northeast edge. Now you would need your own map of Tallinn and the wherewithal to make complex calculations to find the target. Uncommon possessions in the

Middle Ages. Though today Brett's iPad could adjust for scale and fill in the blanks in less than a minute.

And it circled a church.

St Catherine's Dominican Monastery had been built in 1246 and although large parts of it had since fallen into ruin, the refectory, the cloisters, and its gardens had survived. Fortunately. Because according to her calculations, those gardens were her target.

IO

A COLD FOG swamped the morning, shifting on the gusts of wind that periodically bore the scent of salt water and the cries of seagulls from the nearby Baltic. Brett's shoes squeaked on the damp cobbles as she rushed through the old town; her navy blue hoodie and track pants, a concession to function over fashion, were fastened tight against the cold.

Fifteen minutes after leaving her hotel, she turned out of the wind and into a narrow alley squeezed between two rows of slumping medieval buildings; several tiled arches spanned the gap at irregular heights and intervals, serving no clear purpose other than, perhaps, to keep the opposing fieldstone façades apart – if so, they were the prettiest bouncers she had ever seen. Brett pulled a hand-drawn map from her pocket, flattened it on her knee, and flicked the torch between it and the street sign. She was there: St Catherine's Passage.

Gravestones lined the wall a few metres in. They had been moved outside during renovations to the church and had remained there ever since, their inscriptions so shallow now that they were illegible. Brett didn't mind; she was excited by what lay behind them now, not by who had lain below them centuries before, because this was the wall that separated St

Catherine's Passage from the Rectory Gardens. She crept around the corner.

In the pale haze of a streetlight she could make out an arrowhead courtyard and, to her right, a church. She padded closer. She was definitely in the right place: the church's portico was carved with a procession of three dragons. Though roughly rendered and indistinct with age, they undeniably followed each other, nose to tail, into the church. Her Catholic education might have failed to instill any lasting faith, but she was pretty sure that she would have remembered if her catechism classes had mentioned dragons. This was no coincidence. She needed to be in that garden.

The high wall that enforced the garden's perimeter was cut by a slatted metal gate, which a quick investigation revealed to be bolted but unlocked. Brett cringed as its hinges shrieked, but when nobody roused, she slipped into the shadows and latched it closed behind her.

The garden was silent.

She looked around. It was a deep quadrangle, bordered by the church's exterior walls on two sides and by the walls that separated it from the street on the others. Its layout was formal: pebbled paths ran from each corner towards the garden's centre, where they joined and circled a low and wide well. That well was the obvious place to start her search.

It had been constructed from stacked slabs of utilitarian grey stone, chipped and green with moss on its lowest third. Hooding her torch with her hand, she leaned over the lip. The smell of damp air rose lazily from below. She stepped back and looked for another option. The well was probably empty anyway.

Brett walked around the garden, trailing her fingertips along the walls, searching for a clue hidden among the climbing vines or between the rough bricks. She looked back at the well. It took two circuits of the garden to convince her that there was no other option. Then she did a third circuit. Knowing what she had to do – and having the courage to do it – were two different things.

She dragged herself towards the well, stopping a metre away. She shook her head. It was so stupid. She was so stupid. She took a step forward, took three deep breaths, focusing on the oxygen's life giving properties, and peeked in. She cursed herself for waiting. The sun had brightened, revealing even more of the incomplete drop.

Brett retreated. Her heart raced. Her breath came in gasps. It was unreasonable to expect her to climb down a dead end.

This was why she had trained as a marine archaeologist. Her work was seldom more than an exercise in cataloguing the interesting things that had already been pilfered from a wreck, or had decayed to nought, but at least the highest it ever took her was sea level; even when her software business took off, she never rented office space above the ground floor. Brett wiped the sweat from her forehead. She turned back towards the well. From further away it looked less ominous.

Fuck. She sprinted forward. And before she could stop herself, she had pivoted her legs up and over the low wall. She regretted it immediately. Instinct clamped her hands around the stone lip. She hung there, trapped by her fear, until gravity broke the awful equilibrium.

Twenty centimetres of mud and rotting leaves softened her landing, and her torch, which had fallen from her pocket, illuminated weed-penetrated walls of the same grey stone.

Once her heart rate settled, she retrieved the torch and tapped its base against the wall. The wall sounded solid, and as she spun around, looked unbroken except for the small tunnel that must once have brought fresh water in from its source. The tunnel's roof was low and semicircular, its bottom choked with reeking sludge. Brett looked up at her alternative and dropped onto her knees.

She bent forward and, with her arms stretched in front of her and her torch gripped in her mouth, she kicked herself deeper. Then she pulled her knees up and kicked herself deeper again. The tunnel ran for three metres before a chunky iron grate blocked its path. Brett grabbed it and pulled.

There was no movement. She tried again. Nothing. Then she folded her knees under her body, jammed her heels into the walls, and burst forward with a grunt. The bars didn't even rattle.

Brett reversed back into the well, rolled onto her back and reentered the tunnel, feet first this time, and kicked the grate. The extra force made no difference. Not even the second time. Not even the third or fourth.

It was as she slid back, filthy and defeated, that she saw it: a thin bronze band spanning the tunnel's roof, marked by twelve evenly-spaced pictographs.

Brett's hands squelched with childlike enthusiasm. The mud where the band disappeared was gritty with the tunnel's decay but she also felt something bigger, probably a loose stone, though it didn't move when she tugged it. She tugged harder.

With a pop, a bronze nugget the size of a coat button spun free, coming to rest directly above her head. She reached up and slid it down, letting it go and watching as it sprung back to the band's apex. She tested its resistance. Pulling it away from the wall allowed it to be moved along the bronze band, pushing it back in caused it to hold its new position.

Brett was stuck in a stinking well with only half an idea of what to do next, and she was smiling.

II

B RETT TOYED with the nugget while she thought, pressing it into place at each symbol in turn. It only made sense if some pattern of those symbols would open the lock. All she needed then was that pattern. All she needed. . . .

It could be anything.

Except it couldn't be anything. Brett had watched a TV show once where the hero referenced a piece of Buddhist wisdom that said that when you were faced with a seemingly impossible problem, it helped to reverse your thinking and assume you already knew the answer and all that you needed to do was to remember it. It probably wasn't a real Buddhist tenet, but it helped.

There was a solution. There had to be. And it had to be based on logic. More importantly, it had to be based on logic that could be encoded within the clues she already had. Brett thought about possible combinations and tried a few: the dragon first and then the ship; the ship first and then the dragon. Neither worked. She tried the dragon and the fire, and the dragon and the sword, those didn't work either. And they were too simple, anyway. The answer would have to be too complex to be guessed without the clues.

Her fingers hovered over the nugget.

She cocked her head to the side and reconsidered the symbols as a connected thread. Then she dragged the nugget to above the rain cloud. She pushed it home. The tale that had brought her to this well had started with a storm, after all. Brett plucked the nugget out again, hesitated, and dragged it to above the sheep. The people had paid their tribute after the rains, before they found the drowned dragon. So she moved the nugget across to the dragon symbol next, and then to the church. But nothing happened.

She cracked her knuckles.

The story didn't end until the dragon defended Tallinn against the Danish raiding party. Brett slid the nugget across to the sword, and pressed it in.

It was twenty minutes since Brett had opened the grate and, although it was hard to tell how much distance she had covered in that time, little about her surroundings had changed. She was still somewhere under Tallinn. She still had no idea where. Her torch beam was a single stiletto of light, beyond which the darkness was absolute, even the sound of her footsteps seemed to get lost in it. Her morale was threatening to break. She was cold and tired and each new bump hurt more than the one before, each stumble began to feel like a vengeful act wilfully inflicted by the floor. Until something cut the path of her beam.

It was an oak door, its brawn reinforced by three bands of iron; a single keyhole was visible.

Brett reached into her pocket for the keys, but dropped them when her confined world was concussed by noise. She fell to the ground too, cowering as a second shot drowned out her scream. She spun around. She was frantic. And too easy a target kneeling there, exposed and unarmed.

Damn it, she needed the keys.

Prostrate, as if in prayer, she scrambled for – and gratefully found – them.

Sweat poured into her eyes as she flicked through the individual keys, looking for the one she had marked before setting out. She jammed it into the keyhole, turned it, and pushed against the ancient door. The creak of it opening was lost in the thunder of a third shot.

But that shot hadn't come from the tunnel; she now realised that none of them had, they had come from behind the door she was opening.

12

'WHERE DID you get the key?'
It was not what Brett had expected to hear and she
held her punch. She had fallen into a cave whose natural
grittiness had been civilised by the pointed end of a chisel, its
floor tiled over in smooth black and white hexagons. Only its
high ceiling remained a ragged mouth of stalactites, water
dripping from their tips pinged into the receptive puddles that
must have been the source of the room's cold edge.

'Where did you get the key?' The door slammed closed
behind her.

The man addressing her was stocky, not huge but strong
through the chest and shoulders and dressed in an all black
outfit with military styling, though she saw no badges. His
appearance was softened by boyish features and a clump of
dishevelled, sandy-blond hair. Brett ignored his question. She
turned her attention, instead, to the golden relief on the wall
beyond him. It was as wide as the room and taller than her: a
medieval knight standing knee-deep in the sea, battling a
dragon. The knight's sword was raised and his eyes were locked
on the beast, which, equally invested in the fight, had its wings
splayed and its neck recoiled, ready to strike. A pendant hung

at the dragon's chest, an amber sphere that scattered warm light from the torches that burnt along the other walls.

'I asked you where you got this?' He was standing over her now, pushing the key uncomfortably close to her face. She must have left it in the door.

'Give it back to me.'

'Where did you get it?'

'Give it back to me.'

'I'll give it to you when you tell me where the others are.'

Brett rattled her pocket. 'But you're not going to get them.' Despite her tough talk, she hadn't missed the shotgun lying on the camp bed, so she knew that he very easily could get them if he wanted to.

'What? No, not the other keys.' He waved vaguely. 'The others. The other people in your team.'

He stared at her for a silent second, then turned back towards the door and pulled open a spy hole. How had she not seen that earlier?

'Give me back my key.'

'Where are the others?' He turned briefly towards her, then back to the tunnel.

'There are no others, it's only me. It's been only me since the start.'

He blew out a long breath, dropped the key, and kicked it along the floor towards her. 'Did you at least lock the grate when you came in?'

'No. Why would I? I thought that I was the first person down here in hundreds of years. What's going on? Who are you? And, and fuck you, by the way.'

He pinched the bridge of his nose and blinked once, slowly. 'There are more people coming. Six men, according to the security reports. They found the wreck of the *Drachen* a few days ago and were spotted in Tallinn yesterday. That's why I'm down here, waiting.'

'I found the *Drachen.*'

'What?'

'I found the *Drachen,* not them.'

'You're completely missing the point.'

'I'm not. I'm just saying that I found the *Drachen.* Yes, a group of six men knows where the wreck lies, but they didn't find it. I did. They stole it from me.'

'It doesn't matter.'

'It matters to me.'

'Fine. Whatever. You found the *Drachen.* And you found the way here on your own, too?'

'Yes. Mummy says I'm a big girl now.'

'That's not what I meant, but we need to go. Those men will be heading this way soon.'

'No.'

'Oh, for. . . .'

'Why would I go with you? Who are you, even?'

'Can't you hear that?' She could: the faint rhythm of boots striking stone.

'You're asking me to trust you but you won't even tell me your name, or how you got here, or what you want.'

She could hear voices too, now, several voices, getting closer. She held his gaze.

'My name's Sam, Sam Hansen.'

Brett nodded, but she still didn't move.

The footsteps were loud now, rhythmical and precise.

'And I'm a lieutenant-colonel in the British Army; beyond that, you'll need to wait until we have more time. I promise I'll explain everything. We have no other choice. Just . . . have you ever fired a gun?'

'No.'

'Exactly. I'll fire a few shots to unsettle them while you get the dragon. That's what you're after, right?'

Brett had meant 'no, she wouldn't trust him,' though it was also true that 'no, she had never fired a gun'. Now she wasn't sure which interpretation she wanted to stick with.

'Can you pass me the shotgun, please?' Sam was staring through the spy hole. 'They're getting close.'

Then he was screaming at her. She could see his mouth move and his face bluster, though his words were trampled by the ringing in her ears as several guns burst simultaneously to life. His meaning was clear, however. She had to get the gun.

As bullets battered the ancient oak door, Brett sprinted to retrieve the old shotgun. Sam smiled at her, even as wood chips dusted his shoulders and ricocheting shrapnel spat through the opening, and he took the offered gun when she arrived. He loaded two cartridges, lifted the weapon above his head, and fired blindly.

The shotgun was a far cry from the SA80 rifle he used to carry for the British army, but he loved it as he had loved the grandfather who had bequeathed it to him. A weapon with its historical value was just about the only one you could get a licence to transport through Europe these days.

With such a narrow tunnel, it hardly mattered how accurate the old girl was. He fired again.

13

Sam reloaded and fired, reloaded and fired, constructing a rampart of airborne buckshot that held their attackers temporarily at bay. He turned to Brett. 'Get the dragon, you need it and we need to get out of here. I can keep this up for another five minutes, maximum.'

Sam fired another quick salvo and turned back to Brett. She was still there. 'Get the bloody dragon! Either this door is going to shatter or we're going to run out of ammo, but we're not going to win this fight.'

'Why don't you get it and I'll shoot? It's not like I have to aim. And you're taller.'

Sam softened his tone. 'Look, that table there is solid, if you drag it across and stand on it, you won't need to stretch.'

'But ... fine.' Brett scuffed away from the shooting. She pushed the square wooden table against the wall, looked at the carved scene and eased herself up, stomach first, followed by one leg, and then the other, then she rose onto her knees and walked her hands up the wall until she was standing. Her hands searched above her head, and then she found the dragon. She ripped it free and reversed the process until she was sitting on the table with the amber globe held tight in both hands. Her sweaty palms cleared patches in its dusty surface, invigorating its captured light: it was the real thing, though the air was foul with gun smoke and curses so now was not the time to examine it further.

Brett slipped the globe into her bag and jumped off the table. But Sam waved her back as she approached. 'No. Over there. There's another way out and they won't be able to follow us.'

'So what have we been waiting around here for?'

'It's an all or nothing route. It's pretty risky.'

Brett looked him in the eye. 'Explain.'

'There's a second tunnel concealed in the wall. Well, most of a second tunnel. It hasn't been dug all the way through. There are explosive charges embedded in the wall that should complete the job when I set them off, shifting the last two metres of rock from there to here, simultaneously opening up the tunnel for us and blocking their pursuit. That's if it all goes to plan. I think you can imagine how it might not.'

'Set them off.'

Brett crashed headfirst into the ground. As she hauled herself to her knees, a second percussion knocked her straight back down.

When her vision settled, it revealed a changed space, now a little larger than a car garage. Sam stood a metre away, hazy in the rippling dust. 'Sorry, those old charges are unpredictable. We should have had more time than that.'

Brett looked down at her aching body, the thick layer of dust that draped her also helped to stem the bleeding from the two cuts on her right arm. She pointed at the debris behind her. 'It worked, though.'

'It did, indeed. Come.' Sam walked over. As Brett held out her hand, he helped her to her feet. Sam guided Brett through the clutter to where a narrow crack now pierced the far wall.

'Don't worry, it should get wider when we reach the actual shaft.' And with that, he slipped in.

Brett followed him, pushing herself sideways as she'd seen him do. True to his word, minutes later she was breathing cooler air again in a more formally constructed passage.

14

S AM WAS already moving and Brett had to rush to catch up.
The tunnel had been carefully hewn and although it was
still narrow and low, it was roomy compared to the crack they
had just squeezed through; the wooden trusses she tapped as
they passed seemed sturdy despite their age.

They walked, bent over, for fifteen silent minutes until Sam
squatted down at the first corner they encountered. He pulled
a small hand-drawn map from his pocket and held it in the
light. 'It's still a long hike from here, but easy to follow: you go
straight for three miles, turn right at the first opportunity, then
it's another five miles from there, before an open door marks
the final left and a short uphill march to the exit.' The map
disappeared into darkness. Brett looked up just as Sam swung
his torch across, striking her squarely on the temple.

Sam caught Brett's collapsing body in a bear hug and eased
her to the ground, then checked her for a pulse. Good. He
folded the map and placed it next to her unconscious hand,
flicked the torch on and off to test it, and placed it on top like
a paperweight. He rustled through her duffle bag, leaving her
an apple, her wallet, and a small bottle of water, but taking
everything else.

After thirty minutes the tunnel started to change: first bricks appeared, then their colour darkened, then the walls eased apart, and the ceiling rose, blessedly. Sam really had misjudged the force of the explosion and his bruised side and stiff muscles appreciated the opportunity to walk upright again. He maintained his heading for fifteen more minutes, until the tunnel died against a wall.

There he dropped to his knees and fumbled on the ground for a hidden clasp; it was right where his book said it would be. The lock released with a click and the brick wall swung towards him.

Sam propped the secret door open with a brick shard and stepped into a modern storm water drain system. He turned uphill. Soon ladders began to appear; widely spaced, they climbed to the surface through manholes high above his head. He counted the ladders as he passed them, stopping at the fifth one. The tiny eclipse of sunlight that snuck down promised an end to his subterranean jaunt. He tied a piece of string around the ladder's shaft and stepped up.

The rungs were plagued by rust and slick with moss, but they held his weight. Now only a cast iron cover stood between him and fresh air. And soon that was gone.

Sam was lying in a field sprouting cruciform headstones and spring wildflowers, basking in the outdoors as if it were a luxuriant bath. The triangular gable of an abbey cast a shadow from thirty metres away, its ruin a roofless frame for the play of sunlight on its white walls.

St Bridget's Convent had once been the largest nunnery in the region and was still a commanding presence above Pirita Harbour, seven kilometres northeast of central Tallinn. A church had first been proposed for the site by German merchants in 1400, but the project had lacked traction until funds were donated by the Order of Blackheads; funded in secret by the leadership of the Hanseatic League, who were desperate to build a safe link between the Dominican monastery in town, which they already controlled, and their ships that were anchored in the bay. While the contracted workers laid bricks above ground, a second work crew dug the tunnel. Over the years that tunnel had been widened and strengthened and finally linked to the city's plumbing network to hide it in plain sight when its discovery seemed certain.

Sam stripped off his tactical jacket and threw it into his new duffle. He wore a light blue T-shirt underneath; one he had chosen for its cartoon monkey design, which he hoped made him look less threatening and therefore less memorable. But it also felt great to be appropriately dressed for the heat. Springtime in the Baltics seemed designed by a meteorologist with a gambling problem, flipping from hot to cold and back in minutes.

15

THE BOOK that had led Sam to St Bridget's Convent had been accurate, plotting the routes in and out with precision, but he knew it had a dark history. It was almost certainly authored by someone within the secret leadership of the Hanseatic League, but he knew nothing about its provenance prior to it coming into – and quickly out of – the hands of the Nazis, setting into motion the process that he was now bringing to an overdue conclusion.

Sam's grandfather had been a young Lance Corporal when the war reached Norway, but he was intelligent, brave, and fluent in German, and that counted for a lot more than rank. By that time, he knew that the Nazis were fighting an ideological war, not just a military one, and he realised that they wouldn't stop when they had blunted Norway's defences, not even when they had enslaved her people; they would then destroy Norway's culture and usurp it with their own warped icons.

And the most obvious place to start such an attack would be the National Library in Oslo.

Risking a firing squad for breaking curfew, he took up position in the shadows outside a bar, waiting for the right sort of German soldier to walk past, one that was drunk and alone.

He overpowered the man when he came, stole his uniform and, with a commandeered military truck, drove from his home in Bergen to the capital, where he took his biggest risk: dressed in the stolen uniform, he presented falsified orders to the guards stationed outside the library, telling them that he was there to transport the most important books to Berlin. The young guards saw his stripes and jumped into action. As he packed the books into boxes, they even helped to load the boxes into the truck. But the way his grandfather used to tell the story, it was a touch-and-go affair.

'Halt.' He dropped the book he was holding – a biography of Christian Michelsen – and turned. Two soldiers were running towards him. They were no older than him, which meant nothing since in this war everyone was young, but they were running and that was usually a bad sign, and they were dressed in the black uniform of the SS, which always was. 'We were not told about this shipment. Where are you taking those books?'

'These are Norway's books—'

'You're sending them to Germany, yes?'

'Ah, yes. Sir.'

'Under orders from the Reichsführer himself, we have been guarding this book,' he pulled a small, thin bundle from inside his coat, not much more substantial than a few notepad pages cheaply bound together, 'until suitable transport could be arranged to Berlin. We were told the first boat would only be leaving next week; you should have informed us. You will add it to your consignment and you will treat it as a priority item. Guard it with your life.'

'Yes, sir.' They left without acknowledging his salute. And then he took a breath. Why did Heinrich Himmler want these pages so badly? He taped the nearest box closed and, not trusting himself to

maintain the bluff any longer, loaded it into the van himself and drove immediately to the harbour, abandoning hundreds of books to their fate.

A fishing boat was waiting at the dock, fuelled and ready to smuggle the boxes to England. He paid the captain with a case of stolen aquavit and a tug on his patriotic heartstrings, and sent him on his way with a half-full hold.

All those books had made it safely to England, where they sat out the war, before being returned to Oslo. Except for that one, his grandfather had kept that for himself. Anything Heinrich Himmler desired would surely be useful to the resistance.

His grandfather should have been a hero, but that one book made him a laughing stock. It included a map of Tallinn that was drafted in great detail. Which was promising. But it went on to also explain how to break a code embedded in a second book, a code that it said would illuminate the trail to a hidden treasure. That was the clincher.

The obvious assumption was that Himmler already had that second book. And for months they had scanned all Nazi communications, waiting for the code to be used. Waiting for their chance to snatch away the prize.

It never came. The code was never used, never even mentioned.

Eventually he shared the map with the resistance in Tallinn, but although they did find the chamber it pointed to, it was empty.

And still the Nazi chatter never mentioned the book.

In fact, nothing in the book was ever linked to a military purpose and eventually the book became an object of comedy and Sam's grandfather became a target for friendly ridicule:

they started calling him Jack, because he had traded the abandoned books for a handful of beans.

The end of the war presented a final opportunity for redemption, but even then the second book was never found. Of course, many of Himmler's possessions had been burned, looted, or lost, but it hadn't been mentioned in any of his copious records.

Sam's grandfather and his new wife eventually moved to England and since then the little volume had sat dusty on a shelf.

Sam had always loved his grandfather's stories of war and adventure, but it wasn't always obvious that he'd follow him into the military. He had actually been on the far more mundane and lucrative path towards becoming an investment-banking analyst. He had excelled in all things numerical at school and when he was sixteen, he had applied for and won a scholarship to study applied mathematics at the Imperial College London. All he needed to do was pass his A Levels.

A psychologist friend had called it self-sabotage, had said that a fear of failure had led him to scuttle his own dreams, but he knew he'd just taken his foot off the pedal and allowed complacency and an inflated ego to dissolve a long string of class-topping marks into a fail. Like any young man, his first reaction had been to blame everyone else: the exam body that was clearly corrupt, his teachers who were clearly incompetent, and the ancient curse that clearly still heckled his family's name. It took him the better part of a year of pot noodles and cheap beer to grow up. That's when he turned to the military.

What he found was a master that, although intolerant of mistakes on its own watch, was willing to overlook past transgressions. His near record-breaking entrance exam score got him into officer training at the prestigious Royal Military Academy at Sandhurst.

After graduating, Sam served as a tank commander and then, after two highly decorated tours in the Middle East, as a lieutenant-colonel within the Special Reconnaissance Regiment.

It was this last posting that changed things. Up until then, the book had never been able to lead him beyond the same empty chamber below the monastery. In his new role, though, while he continued to loyally serve his queen and country, the intelligence gathering systems he had access to allowed him to reinvigorate the hunt.

It took another year to link the chamber under the monastery and its single amber globe to the larger story; and even then, it had simply gotten him one step further down the trail.

What he did know, though, was that if the second book existed, anyone who followed its path would, at some point, be led to Tallinn. So he had left the globe there and waited.

Patience; patience; patience; and now, finally, reward.

Sam held the coded map to the treasure that would exalt his family name. He was tempted to open the book right there, but the nearby sound of laughter reminded him of how exposed he was. He glanced around: just a harmless blend of mothers with young children and camera-laden tourists. The laughter had come from two youths with Boston Red Sox caps pulled low, who were walking his way, no doubt looking for a shady spot to sleep off the night before.

When they passed, he was alone.

16

WHAT SAM hadn't told Brett was that there was a number carved into the wall of the cavern. This number referred to the page in the book where the next hiding place's tale began. It also marked the spot where the fuses for the explosive charges were buried so that, should the need ever arise, the trail could be severed. As Sam had done.

For years he'd sat, like some re-imagined Cassandra, knowing that he must turn to page eighty-two, but not having the pages. He smiled. He finally knew where he was going next and, just as importantly, Brett did not. That smile died as he looked up.

The two youths had turned and were running towards him.

Sam jumped up, grabbed the bag, tossed the book in, and ran the other way.

Five steps later he spun on his heels and headed back towards the youths, because four other men were coming from the parking lot with guns drawn. Also, as long as he was between the two groups, neither would be able to open fire for fear of hitting the other.

When the two youths were ten metres away, Sam shoved his right hand into the duffle bag, found his shotgun, and without taking it out he fired. The youths hit the ground, and he leapt over their prone bodies, firing a second time to keep them down. And then sprinted for all he was worth. He had escaped the frying pan, but without the cover the youths had provided, he might have landed in the fire. It was too late to question his strategy, and certainly too late to change it – he stood no chance in a six-against-one gunfight – so he kept running.

The path climbed uphill and away from the abbey, ending at an observation deck that presented tourists with serene harbour views and presented him, he hoped, with a fast route down into the suburbs. He had 400 metres to cover before he'd know for sure.

Sam was through the first fifty of those metres and no shots had been fired. So the youths had been unarmed, but the second group would be in a shooting position soon.

He had actually covered another fifty metres when that first shot did come, but the shooter had used his time well and was on target immediately: the sleeve of Sam's shirt tore open at the same time he heard the bang.

He dodged right.

A second shot flew past, then a third, which was close enough to warm the air. He dodged right again. Then he dodged left.

He wasn't yet half way.

The fourth and fifth shots were further off. But the sixth shot exploded in a recent footprint. And the seventh shot found its mark. Searing pain sliced through Sam's calf and he crashed to the ground.

The eighth, ninth, and tenth shots followed in quick succession; all too high as Sam fumbled in the bag. He pivoted and fired both barrels, buying time.

And then he was moving again.

The red brick boundary wall was close now, peaks of thin spruce trees visible just beyond it, suggesting a manageable drop on the other side. More shots came – now in bursts aimed with less care – and the ground to his right erupted in mini volcanoes. He stepped that way and the next volley struck far to his left. His final hurdle was now just thirty metres away.

The shots were desperately frequent now, though Sam no longer paid any attention to where they were striking. Close, he knew. His lungs were burning. His heart was at the point of rupture. The wall in front of him broke out in polka dots. Thin cracks sped between the bullet holes, and larger pieces of masonry chipped free. And then he was there.

Sam vaulted the wall and hit the ground hard on the other side. He tumbled, uncontrolled and too fast, snatching at bushes as they buzzed past, tearing leaves and hands as he burst through them, until the coarse terrain bled enough of his speed to bring him back to rest.

Shaken, scratched, bruised, and bleeding, he looked back up the hill as six heads peered over the wall, and then disappeared just as quickly. Police sirens were now whining in the distance, reminding him that he needed to leave, too.

Sam pushed himself up and dusted his hands on his ruined pants. Although everything hurt, the damage was manageable. Half limping and half sliding, he made his way down to the harbour.

17

B RETT FORCED her eyelids apart. It was a wasted effort; she couldn't see anything. She couldn't hear anything, either, except for the low throb of her headache. She lay like that for a minute, fuming. That bastard had hit her. She would get him for that.

Her hands scrabbled around, knocking against a torch, which she grabbed and switched on. In its beam she saw that he had stolen her bag, too, leaving her with nothing but her wallet and an apple – her own fucking apple. No, she would not accept this.

The stupid thing was that she didn't particularly care about the treasure. She was rich already. More than rich enough, anyway. Much more. In fact, that was her main headache. After she had sold her business, she had begun to drift; she hadn't wanted to get back into teaching, hadn't wanted to start another business, hadn't wanted to do any of the things she could now afford to do. And her marine archaeology work had dried up the moment she became an IT entrepreneurial success story. Her life was like one of those rooms featured in interior decorating magazines: enviable and glamorous when viewed from the outside but empty and pointless when actually experienced. She had needed an impetus to escape from that luxurious quicksand.

Her catalyst had come in the form of a mythological shipwreck, a fringe theory rejected by historians but so reminiscent of her late dad's flights of fancy that she'd felt compelled to pursue it. She had started the search for the *Drachen* as a way to remember him and as a way to get back her zest for life.

And she had.

The day when she first saw that angular beam poking through the sandy seabed had been an affirmation. She had been ecstatic. So of course, it had been an anticlimax when she cut into the *Drachen* and found its hold empty. But she would have been willing to accept that as a lesson in valuing the journey above the destination; a chapter end and a chance to start afresh.

Until someone had tried to take it away from her.

And now it was happening again. She wasn't going to let Sam do that. She wasn't going to let anyone do that.

Brett polished the apple and took a hungry bite, then unfolded the paper upon which it had rested. It wasn't an apology note – it was the map from earlier. Did Sam think she was an idiot?

She stood up, waited for the dizziness to subside, and started to walk.

The tunnel ended at a ladder that disappeared into blinding sunlight. She took three deep breaths and put her foot on the first rung, took three more breaths and put it back on the floor. She looked up. Thought about the fresh air, thought about retribution, and then, with her eyes locked on the skyline, she started to climb.

A minute later, she lay among wildflowers in the grounds of a ruined church, savouring the sweet air in decadent breaths. But she didn't have time to rest. Brett stood up, tied her filthy hoodie around her waist, and walked towards the church's parking lot. She had to get back to the hotel.

The sky was an institutional grey, from corner to corner without variation. Like it had been painted by an accountant. Hiko's mood was equally bland. He was sitting on the deck of his fireboat, bouncing a tennis ball and waiting. This time his phone rang right on time. 'You've got good news?'

'It's too early to say, but it's not bad news, sir.'

He waited. That didn't warrant a compliment.

'The divers retrieved traces of organic matter, sir.'

'Viable samples?'

'We're testing it all, but after so long in sea water, I am not sure how much it will give us. It's a step forward, though.'

'At the moment it doesn't sound like much of anything.'

'There is a little more. We've identified some unique markers in the DNA.'

'And?'

'At this stage "unique" is a very good sign. This is a new thing, something against which medical science won't yet have a defence.'

'You're still studying the samples?'

'Yes.'

The bed that had felt so uncomfortable the night before was now a sanctuary as Brett sank under the covers, still in her muddy track pants.

She woke an hour later with a start. She wasn't going to run away from this or stand still while it ran away from her, but she needed help, and that fact didn't make her any weaker.

Brett reached for her phone and listened to several far away rings before a jovial voice answered amidst a babble of background noise.

'Patrick?'

'Brett, I haven't seen you in ages, not since that whole karaoke debacle. We must do that again.'

Brett laughed at that memory, surprising herself. 'Patrick, as I recall, halfway through confessing your undying love for me you started talking about the rugby, and then halfway through that story you switched tables to flirt with a pretty blonde. I think you left without saying good bye to anyone and I had to pay your tab.'

'Ha, ha. You're right, I did do that. And my song choice that night was terrible, but I have fixed that, out with the old and in with the new. No more *Country Roads* for me, I've been doing a lot of Emeli Sandé recently; very contemporary; very edgy for a male artist.'

'Patrick—'

He broke into song.

'Stop, stop, stop. That's awful. And that's also not why I called.'

'Oh, God, is it about that whole "undying love" thing? I was kidding. Unless. . . .'

'Patrick, I need your help.'

He stopped and listened as she explained her story.

'Obviously I'll do everything I can, but I'm not sure how much that is. This is beyond my field of expertise.'

'Patrick.'

'I'm serious. I'm just an architect.'

'Yes, but you know you know ... things.' She waved her hands in an all-encompassing gesture that she knew he couldn't see.

'Is that old story still kicking about? It's not true. It doesn't matter; of course, I'll come over and do whatever I can. But I'm just saying. Give me some time to find a flight and I'll send you the details.'

18

TALLINN'S Central Bus Station was too plain to be called ugly. It was just a cement rectangle housing ticket offices for each of the three major bus lines, a canteen-quality restaurant, shabby public toilets, and nothing more. Behind the off-white building, six covered platforms provided wisps of shade for the disorganised mass of waiting passengers.

Sam had bought a ticket to Riga, on a bus leaving in half an hour. He would be there four hours after that, early enough to start his search before nightfall.

The tide of passengers ebbed and flowed with the departure and arrival of buses and all the while Sam slouched among the throng, keeping an eye out for anyone who might be paying him a little too much attention. There was nothing out of the ordinary. When his bus did arrive, it was a modern one, which was a relief since some of those heading to lesser destinations looked overworked and under maintained.

Sam was the last to board. He had paid the small premium for first class, which granted him a muesli bar, a bottle of water, and a semblance of legroom in a section at the very back of the bus; there, he joined a young American couple and an older man who was already buried in his newspaper.

Although the bus was advertised as 'express' to Riga, the driver made a handful of stops along the way: the first was five minutes into the trip when a hooting taxi overtook the bus and waved it to a stop, allowing a plump and embarrassed woman to scramble aboard; the second an hour later near a petrol station, where a middle-aged man carrying four shopping bags got off and disappeared; and the final stop came a kilometre after the border crossing, where a man wearing a Boston Red Socks baseball cap flagged them down from the thin shade of a road sign.

He boarded the bus and walked down the aisle, glancing left and right. Sam slid deeper into his seat.

Then the young man stopped, threw a small backpack into the overhead tray, and took a seat four rows in front of the first class section; he pushed his chair into a shallow recline, pulled his cap down over his eyes, and promptly fell asleep.

That upgrade had just paid for itself. Sam knew that if he hadn't been spotted by the young man yet, stopping the bus to get off would guarantee that he was. But it was much more likely that Sam had already been spotted, probably in Tallinn, and that the youth was just his babysitter; that would explain the silver BMW trailing a few hundred metres behind the bus. If that was the case, staying on until Riga was the bigger risk.

Sam slipped his phone from his pocket and tapped in a number he hadn't used for years. It was time for plan C.

A minute later he put his phone away and watched the empty flatness of Latvia trundle past – lots of fields, some trees, and a few worn houses. Riga was less than fifty kilometres away and he could do nothing now but wait.

The bus rounded a bend and dove into a jolting stop, joining the queue of cars seething behind a black Ford Focus stationary in the middle of the road with its emergency lights flashing. The Ford's owner was wearing an expression that mixed frustration and embarrassment, a look familiar to any man forced to publicly admit that he has no idea how to repair his own car. But he was also a big, tattooed man and it was perhaps because of that, rather than out of empathy, that the other cars held their silence.

Sam was out of his seat in an instant, running forwards.

The youth in the baseball cap was rising, too, and pulling a phone from his pocket. Sam grabbed it with his left hand as he ran past, and punched with his right as the boy turned in protest. The punch wasn't hard, but it came as a surprise and was enough to knock him back down.

'Open the door! Open the door!' Sam tossed a crumpled note at the driver in case there were any issues with translation, and ducked out as the doors rocked open.

The Ford's driver had abandoned his charade the second the bus stopped. He slammed the bonnet closed and was behind the wheel when Sam opened the passenger door. The car was in gear as Sam slid into the deep bucket seat, and the tyres were spinning by the time he slammed the door.

Sam turned back to watch the action behind them. The youth from the bus was standing in the road, hands on narrow hips, nose bleeding, watching their escape. He let out a yell and then jogged back to the BMW. A second later it rocketed onto the road's verge and began its pursuit amid a hail of gravel.

Sam turned back to the driver and smiled, 'Hey Roman, thanks for coming.' Though the heavy bass beats that were pounding his back probably rendered his greeting as inaudible as Roman's reply. Sam gestured for the volume to be lowered, but Roman shook his head. 'Car chase music,' he yelled back.

19

MATTHYS PUSHED back his keyboard and ate absent-mindedly as he stared at his screen. He had a lead. It wasn't a very good lead, but it was more interesting than the statistics that he was supposed to be compiling on the risks smuggled cigarettes posed to public health.

A man in Estonia had responded to one of the adverts he'd sprinkled through various art publications. He had wanted to know if Matthys would also be interested in an artwork that was dragon related. The man said he owned a painting, the remaining half of a pair, that depicted a sailing ship whose figurehead was a dragon. He had actually been a very good salesman. Apparently the painting in question was a study of that figurehead – done to full scale if you allowed yourself to get caught up in his hyperbole. A carved beast plated in greening copper clutched the front of a ship, its wings extended, its neck twisted so its head faced forward, flaring its nostrils and bearing a double row of gold teeth.

Matthys had been intrigued by the words 'one half of a pair'. In fact, he had been so intrigued that he had bought the piece. Yet, even though the painting had cost him a week's wages, his focus was on the tidbit of information that had come contingent to the deal: the name and phone number of the buyer of the companion piece.

The other painting had been purchased three months previously by a young Italian woman searching for medieval artworks and books featuring this particular dragon-adorned ship. Matthys checked the clock. He was waiting to call her again but it had been fourteen minutes since his last unsuccessful attempt to reach her and this time he had promised himself he would wait for a full half hour.

Her choice of painting was intriguing. There was that word again. It was a dangerous word, a word that might well be his downfall, but it was also an apt word, because she had bought the wrong painting.

One painting showed the ship's most prominent feature in glorious and lifelike detail – or so he hoped, since he now owned it – while the other showed the ship at a distance, obscured by the smoke and shrapnel of a sea battle. So why would someone who was actively searching for pictures of the ship buy the latter instead of the former?

Matthys stared at the scanned photograph of the painting he didn't own and searched for meaning. Then he checked the clock again.

20

ROMAN HAD been born in Moldova and it was there that he had learned how to fight and how to drink, which meant he really knew how to fight and really, really knew how to drink – and he had done both side-by-side with Sam. The two men first met during NATO joint operations in the Middle East and had worked together several times since. Today, Roman was wearing a luminous green vest; the thick arms it revealed were decorated with Cyrillic tattoos of varying quality and his head had been shaved smooth above a thick black beard. But despite his hard looks, his smile was easy and repeated in his brown eyes.

'Can we outrun them?' Sam threw a thumb in the direction of the silver BMW.

'We've got more power and less weight, but that doesn't even matter. I could outrun them if I was driving that bus you rode in on.'

Roman turned back to watch the road. The curbside trees blurred into a single hazy entity and the engine growled with added ferocity. A minute later they were in the oncoming lane as he searched for the racing line around a tight right-hand bend; it was like living in a David Guetta music video.

Despite Roman's swagger, the BMW was still there, a hundred metres behind. 'Do not worry, Sam, do not worry.'

Roman was the embodiment of his own advice: one hand drummed on the steering wheel while the other alternated between expert gear shifts and awful dance moves. In fact, he was so into the music that he didn't flinch at the first gunshot. Sam did. He spun around and saw a gun flashing out of the passenger side of the BMW. The second shot came during a lull in the music and Roman heard that one. He jigged the car left and right.

'Roman?'

The world exploded in a cloud of feathers and surprised birds as Roman swung the car off the road and straight through a chicken coop, cutting deep troughs in the grass as he bullied them in the direction of a farmstead and the road that was visible just beyond it.

The BMW flew past in a protest of brake noise and rubber smoke.

Seconds later, Roman ramped up onto the dirt road, still at full throttle. Its surface was true, though Sam doubted Roman would have driven any differently if it hadn't have been.

The flat countryside vibrated as patches of pasture and clumps of thin trees sped past, split by occasional driveways, but never another road. Roman didn't seem to be concerned and he kept the speed relentlessly high. The BMW driver seemed less confident and the gap between the two vehicles slowly began to grow.

'Where are we?' Sam shouted when the BMW slipped from view.

'I don't know. Sometimes you have to improvise.'

Sam had feared that answer. He tapped Roman on the shoulder and pointed forward. 'See that farmer up there, what's he driving?'

Roman shrugged. 'A tractor probably. Pile of junk certainly, no point in jacking it, if that's what you're thinking.'

'Bloody hell, why would we . . . never mind. No, I meant that cloud of dust behind it. So let's get in it and, when we're hidden by a rise or something, pull off and hide in the trees. Hopefully those guys will keep following the cloud, giving us a chance to head back to the main road once they pass. By the time they catch the farmer, we'll be long gone.'

Roman nodded, and somehow whipped even more power from the engine.

'That's not what I meant!'

Roman had just slammed the wheel hard left, taking the car airborne.

The shock absorbers echoed Sam's complaints a second later as they crashed down, but Roman kept his foot flat.

The wheels spun through dirt and grass, fighting for grip.

The car lurched sideways.

Trees rushed towards them.

Roman over-corrected their skid and suddenly, they were facing backwards. The first tree whipped past like that. More trees came in a flurry. They lost a wing mirror. Flattened a sapling. Glanced off a thicker trunk. Lost the other wing mirror. Roman's hands and feet were still working overtime when they finally bumped to a stop, a ticker tape of leaves and twigs celebrating their somewhat safe arrival.

'That should do it.' Roman blinked twice and then kicked the door open and got out to inspect the damage. 'Nothing a day at the panelbeaters can't fix. Anyway, you look well, old friend.'

Forty seconds later, the silver BMW sped past. Roman waited another thirty seconds to be sure, and then eased the dented Ford back through the trees. 'Well, who would have guessed?' he said. 'There might be something to this planning thing, after all.'

21

ROMAN SWUNG onto the tarmac without concession to oncoming traffic and pumped the weary accelerator, unwilling to give the BMW even the slightest opportunity to catch up. It worked; the only object in the rearview mirror remained the fuzzy cherries Roman had stuck there as a memento from his most recent trip to Ibiza.

It was twenty minutes until Roman relented, slowing down to ninety kilometres an hour as he turned into a bland suburban street. Three anonymous streets later, they pulled to a stop outside a grey tower block. Roman hooted twice, rousing a young man in dirty overalls who dragged open the razor-wire-topped gate and waved them in. Roman parked around the back and hid the car beneath a dusty canvas cover, then ushered Sam into the building and, via a decrepit elevator, to his apartment.

'Thank you.' Sam took a cold beer from Roman and they tapped bottles. 'And for fetching me.'

The apartment was furnished entirely from Ikea by the looks of it, but from the top end of their range: lots of black and white and clean Nordic lines. The room's colour came in splashes of red, yellow, and silver from the framed posters that lined the wall, all of supercars, most with their engines exposed. Roman waved away Sam's gratitude. 'I had lots of fun. And, I think I still owe you a few favours from the old days. But what is our next step? I assume we're in Riga for a reason?'

'Tell me how, Kalev.'

'We had a man on the bus, two following in the car, and four each at both of the drop off points in Riga; we had all the escape routes covered.'

'It sounds like you are telling me exactly how he *didn't* escape, Kalev, when patently he did.'

Hiko kept his voice calm. Soothing even. He didn't need to shout. In fact, it was better that he didn't. Just hearing his own name, repeated like that, would send shivers down Kalev's spine. His mum had taught him that trick.

Kalev and Hiko had never met in person – a necessary concession to the machismo of men of Kalev's ilk, few of whom would take orders from a petite man just out of his teens – but Kalev was scared of Hiko. Hiko knew that. Kalev was right to be scared, of course. Hiko could do a lot of damage to Kalev. He could also reward Kalev exponentially. Well beyond the million euros Kalev had found in his account after Hiko's envoy first contacted him.

'We were outmanoeuvred, sir. It was an error in planning, not in execution, so I have to take the blame.'

So Kalev had fallen on his sword. He had surely considered lying. Considered selling out his men. Anyone would have. And Hiko doubted it was loyalty to them that had stopped him. Kalev just wasn't an idiot. He knew that a discovered lie would carry severe sanction.

'Kalev, I'm not looking to blame anyone. I just want to make sure we put an end to this.'

'Yes, sir.' Hiko loved hearing that 'sir'.

'Good. I want your men watching all the noteworthy buildings in Riga. When they spot him, and I want them to spot him by the end of tomorrow, they must grab him and take him somewhere secure. Then I want you to call me.'

'Yes, sir.' There it was again.

Roman had left twenty minutes ago with a list of supplies they didn't really need. Sam had brought out the book and the keys the moment the door closed and he was still studying them now. He wanted Roman's help, but it was too soon to put all of his cards on the table.

So far he'd sketched a simple map of Riga – a broken rectangle, topped with a Y-shaped fork – and matched it to the block of the Old Town that ran from the river to the town square. He was using the instructions in his grandfather's book. Or rather, his grandfather's book was useful – and that was a huge relief. Some roads were different today but enough of the old lanes lined up to reassure him. A small gold cross marked the location of St Peter's Church, the 800-year-old building whose cockerel weather vane was something of a symbol of the city. It was the obvious hiding place. Except that he knew that it wasn't.

Now, following the book's instructions, Sam examined the keys he'd taken from Brett and selected the right one; he calculated the amount of white space it traversed, adjusted for the scale, and compared the point it now circled to a tourist map: St John's Church.

He grabbed a guidebook.

The history of St John's was vague and promising. It had been built in the late thirteenth century, by the Dominicans again, and was most famous for the story of the two monks who were said to have lived their entire adult lives bricked within its walls.

It had to be the place.

Sam sat back in the chair and sipped his beer, glad to be out of the soaking rain that had begun to fall.

22

PATRICK CHECKED the address and rang the bell.

He crept deeper into his mint blazer as a stiff breeze tousled his curly brown hair. His face was covered in five-day stubble which, despite having been around for considerably less time than the hair on his head, was already primarily grey. With the way his green eyes and dimples conspired, Patrick always looked like he was midway through a particularly funny story, but his smile really stretched his cheeks as he reminisced about how he and Brett had met.

'Run!' That had been his first word to her. And to her credit, it had only taken her a second to react.

He'd seen her standing outside a jewellery store staring wistfully at a watch in the window. Looking very sad. Looking very beautiful. And that's where fate had played the role it so often did in life, because he had just signed a career-defining deal that day. He was feeling very rich. And a little drunk. So he'd gone into the shop and bought the watch. But he'd asked the salesman to leave the security tag on.

A second after he slapped the watch into Brett's hand the shop's alarm had pealed, and that's when he'd shouted at her to run. She'd followed him for three blocks before they slowed to a stop outside a romantic little pub he knew.

They had been friends ever since, and to this day, she wore that watch. Though he had never worked up the courage to tell her the truth.

The creak of the floorboards brought him back to the present, and a second later Brett was pulling open the door. They embraced.

'Thank you. I'm so glad to see you. Come in. Come in. We're through there. I'll bring a stool. This is Rasmus, it's his house, he's helping me with some background information.'

'Welcome, Patrick, and thank you, I believe you're here to help us,' Rasmus said.

'I'll do what I can. Lovely jumper, by the way.' Patrick could charm the birds out of the trees.

Rasmus looked down and smiled. 'Thank you. And what is it that you do, if I may ask?'

'I'm an architect.'

Brett shot him a look.

'It's true.' He did his best to imitate her angry-teacher stare, eliciting reluctant giggles from Brett. He turned back to Rasmus. 'Sorry. Yes, I'm an architect, it's just that some of my friends prefer not to believe me. You see, I specialise in national monuments and governments that are in the market for national monuments have often recently emerged from rough transitions so, from time to time, my work puts me in contact with people and situations that are . . . unusual. But I'm Brett's friend and that's why I'm here, qualified for the role or not.'

'Good enough for me. Coffee?'

'A beer would be great, thanks. Guinness if you have, though Saku is perfect, too.'

By the time Brett had rehashed the previous day's events, Patrick was looking concerned. 'So, do we know where the next of these dragons is, then?'

Brett looked at Rasmus and he shook his head. 'Brett and I have made a few guesses. It's no secret where the Hansa had their strongholds at the time, so those towns would be our starting point.'

'Brett, do you have anything left: copies of what Sam stole, or anything that might help us to narrow down the search?' Patrick asked.

'Just snippets on the iPad. Here, have a look, it'll give you an idea of what we're talking about. There's definitely too little information to identify the next town, though.'

'You thought the same about Tallinn until not too long ago. Come, I've got fresh eyes. Now, you said the treasure was hidden and that the *Drachen* was sent to deliver its clues, right?'

'Right.'

'Well, if the first clue was the dragon that you found on the wreck, and the second clue was the one you found in Tallinn, then even if we can't identify the hiding place of the third dragon, maybe we can just jump ahead and identify the hiding place of one of the other dragons. They must lie west of here, surely? And near the coast.'

It often amazed Brett how Patrick switched so easily from a laid-back charmer to a focused analyst when there was work to be done.

'We thought of that already: Riga, Rostock, Lübeck, Visby, Hamburg, Brussels, or even Bergen, and a few smaller places in between fit that bill.' Brett looked at Rasmus for reassurance. He nodded.

'Exactly.'

'Well, how did you know there was one here in Tallinn?'

'Huh, we didn't even think of that. Dumb luck, I guess.'

'Excellent, then we play the hot streak and pick one.'

'It doesn't work like—'

'Lübeck.' Brett was cut off and all eyes turned to Rasmus.

'We don't know that. If we go to the wrong town, we could waste days on a wild goose chase while they're finding my treasure,' Brett said.

'I know. Still, if we have to pick one town, we should pick Lübeck. For sure. It's the only one I'm certain they'll go to. It was called the Queen of the Hanseatic League and it was the *Drachen's* home port. It has to be on the route. Has to be. Also, given the location of the wreck there is only really one place it could have been taking the last clue: Visby. And that with would be consistent with a circular route heading east out of Lübeck and back from the north.'

'Fine. Lübeck then, but how do you know the others haven't already been there?' Patrick asked.

'Obviously I don't, but if you go straight away they'll have, at most, a two-day head start. So even if they did go straight there, you could still catch them.'

'And we have no idea where to look once we're there?' Patrick looked at Rasmus and then at Brett. They both shook their heads. 'Never mind, it's a start. I'll phone and book us three tickets on the first flight out.'

'Just two tickets.'

'What? No, you're part of this too.' Brett said. 'You've always believed in the *Drachen,* haven't you? Isn't this what you always dreamed of?'

'It is. Or it was. Well, it still is but I'm too old now, Brett. You went on your own yesterday because, consciously or subconsciously, you knew that to be true.'

'I'm sorry.'

'Don't be. It was the right decision. You say I always believed in the *Drachen* and that is true. I never acted though, like you are now. You're not taking my chance from me now. I missed it years ago. Tell me what you find, though, please. And let me help as much as I can before you go.'

23

WITHOUT A CENTRAL hill upon which to sit, Riga was less dramatic than Tallinn, though it felt more lived in, even this early in the morning when the streets were almost empty. Sam and Roman were walking towards St John's Church, excitement overcoming their lack of sleep.

St John's lay on the outskirts of the Old Town, near where the city wall had once run. Its red brick walls were stocky, built on the original foundations of a castle, and topped by a typical stepped façade. Once again the Hansa had eschewed the most imposing building in town – St Peter's had a taller tower and was more dramatically framed by a paved piazza – in favour of one that exuded charm from every pore.

Sam was dressed in head-to-toe black again, while Roman wore blue and grey camouflage fatigues he'd won off a Captain in the Russian Spetsnaz during a vodka-addled poker game. Roman had copied Sam and stripped the uniform of all insignia, and had stocked the combat harnesses they both wore with essential tools of the burglary trade. He had, however, been unable to acquire further firepower so the only weapons they carried were Sam's old shotgun and a brace of knives apiece.

They tried the most obvious entry point first, but the front doors were locked. A sign on the wall listed the opening times: not until 07:00. It was probably for the best, since they didn't want anyone there to witness their search.

A narrow lane ran between the church and its neighbours, circling the building. Several auxiliary doors opened onto the path, but those were locked too. They wouldn't be difficult to pick, but Roman and Sam were looking for a less obtrusive means of entry, if possible.

It was Roman who spotted it.

A gnarled tree grew there, so close to the church's front wall that it might have sprung from a seed dropped into the foundations when the first stones were laid. The tree's lowest branches were easily reachable and soon Roman was perched alongside an unlocked first-storey window. He leant his shoulder against it. He leant a little harder to overcome years of rust, and though it creaked with reluctance, the window opened.

The interior was cool and still, with a sillage of rich incense. A narrow ledge ran along the wall, five metres above the floor. With Roman leading the way, they edged towards the choir stall.

From there, a wooden staircase took them down to the nave.

'So, what are we looking for?' Roman's whisper echoed like a sermon, startling both men.

'I'm not sure, something that looks out of place, or something that looks like it could be related to the *Drachen*: a dragon or a ship, maybe. Hopefully we'll know it when we see it.'

The nave was a nest of columns and shadows. Every surface was covered in religious engravings and gilt-framed iconography, every piece of furniture was intricately carved; it would be a long search. Sam handed Roman a torch and they split up:

Roman would concentrate on the paving stones, in case a message had been laid out in their geometric patterns, while Sam would search the south wall, where the monks had allegedly been bricked in. Perhaps that legend had evolved from a true story of clandestine construction work.

Roman gave up on the floor after twenty minutes. Any clue so subtle as to be invisible to him would also have been lost in the many renovations made to the church since the Hansa had left; and anyway, what Sam was doing looked more interesting. He walked to where Sam was staring at a paperback-sized icon on a pillar. 'What's so special about this one?'

Sam didn't have time to answer.

They both spun around: a key was turning in the front door's lock. They killed their torches and ducked behind the closest pillar. A second later, the heavy door scraped along the flagstone floor.

It wasn't a diligent priest.

Three men stepped through the door, two carrying metal trunks behind another who scanned the space with a raised assault rifle. Their faces were anonymously hard. Military types for sure. They looked around and waved in a fourth man who pulled the door closed behind him, but not before more shadows were visible outside. This last man seemed inappropriately dressed for the occasion; he wore a silver pinstripe suit that, except for where the outline of a gun spoiled the effect, made him look like a self-consumed investment banker. He was stick thin too, or perhaps his height exaggerated the illusion, because he must have stood two metres tall. By the way the others deferred to him, it was clear that he was the leader.

Sam slipped off his boots, Roman mimicked him, and on stockinged feet they crept back up to the choir stall. From there they watched torch beams sweep the room in a coordinated search. A moment later, the church was filled with tepid yellow light as the main switches were found. These visitors were staying.

24

FULL LIGHT was still an hour away, and the four men were searching the church with a level of industry that suggested they wanted to be gone by then. They had connected a laptop to something that looked like a boxy sci-fi ray gun, which they used to take readings at intervals along the wall, pausing periodically to review the data. The church's acoustics broadcast the men's conversations clearly; they were searching for a weak spot.

Relying on their shared military past, Sam and Roman conferred with hand signals. Roman's plan was to attack immediately, surprising the men while they were still in a research mindset. Sam shook his head, tapped his watch, and signalled that he wanted to wait for the four men to find whatever it was they were looking for. They were still gesturing back and forth when the wall exploded. Providence had provided a third option.

The explosion had sent a thick crack running through the mortar, framing a low and narrow rectangle. Two men strode through the settling dust wielding long-handled hammers, and with three swift blows they had knocked through an opening. They stepped back to let the leader through, and then followed him in.

When Sam and Roman reached the ground floor, the fourth man was packing away the equipment alone. They were on him before he knew what was happening: he tried to turn, but all he would have seen was the briefest flash of Roman's fist.

Ten seconds later, he was unconscious on the floor, tightly bound and gagged. Sam and Roman rolled his limp body under a pew, pulled their boots back on, and headed to the hole in the wall.

The space they entered was just a gap: fifty centimetres of space between the internal and external walls that they would have assumed had been set aside for cables and ducting if it was in a modern building.

Though the gap extended in both directions, they could hear muffled voices receding to the left. They followed the sound as quickly as they could manage, though as the light faded away, it became a progressively slower and more painful task. For the first five minutes the voices continued to recede, even as Sam and Roman moved deeper; then the voices started to get louder. The men must have stopped.

Sam and Roman stopped, too, then moved forward with even more caution. Fragments of light appeared and brightened. The tunnel turned and twenty metres later, it ended in a crowded nook.

Elongated sentry shadows patrolled its uneven walls. The nook was lit by twin halogen spotlights, both aimed at a bronze disk in the floor, which sparkled under their glare. The disk was the size and shape of a manhole cover, and decorated with a bass relief that was too far away for them to see clearly. Two of the men were pacing around it while the leader was kneeling close, apparently caressing its surface. They had to get a closer look.

'Stop.' Sam and Roman froze. 'I can't see a damn thing with you idiots moving in front of the lights.' The two soldiers stopped and Sam and Roman edged forward again.

The leader beckoned one of his men closer and rose. Although Sam and Roman couldn't hear the subsequent conversation, it was clear from the tone and his body language that he was frustrated. With a curse, he turned and headed back towards the church, his two lieutenants a step behind.

Panic filled the constricted space as Sam and Roman scrambled for a plan. They had the old shotgun and twelve cartridges, too little firepower given the guns they'd seen the three men carrying: even if Sam managed to fire off both barrels, he'd never get the chance to reload. They couldn't run, either. The three men with their torches would be able to move much quicker than Sam and Roman could.

Their survival would depend on a massive dose of luck. In some places the walls were so close that you had to walk sideways, in other sections there was enough space for a collegial conversation; most importantly, though, there was no obvious pattern to the variation. Sam and Roman dropped to the floor, rolled into two indentations provided by such inconsistencies, and stretched themselves as long and as flat as possible. They hushed their breathing, hoping the three men would be too preoccupied to spot them as they marched past.

To give themselves the best chance, they had hidden just beyond the range of the halogen lights, where the darkness of the tunnel would appear to be at its deepest to the approaching men's unaccustomed eyes.

Roman watched the first silhouette, tall and thin, step out of the light. The man stumbled forward, his hands thrust out before him like an actor hamming up the role of a risen-from-the-dead mummy. Heavy boots stomped closer. The dust they disturbed settled on Roman's cheek. Roman could hear the man's breathing, could hear hands slapping the rock face, could hear his own heart beating loud and fast in his chest. He tried to force it slower: one, one thousand, two, one thousand, three, one thousand, and then the man was gone. Then Roman heard the man fumbling with something, saw the spark of a torch turning on; but by that time the man was already five metres down the tunnel and no longer a threat. One down, two to go. He had no chance to catch his breath. Here they came: the remaining two men were approaching together, evenly, unaware. Then the man in front struck his shin against a spur of rock and came to a cursing stop.

He shook his head like an irritated buffalo. Drops of his sweat splashed onto Roman's arm. He pushed himself even flatter against the unyielding wall.

The man patted his pockets. 'Can I borrow your torch? I left mine back there.'

'Aw, did you hurt you widdle legsies? Move it, Kalev won't wait.'

The man grunted and trudged forwards. His colleague followed behind him, keeping his torch spitefully stowed, chuckling at each subsequent collision.

Sam and Roman flopped back into the passage and rushed towards the lit chamber. They had very little time and they had burned their own boats. Once the three men found their bound comrade, they would summon backup and then they'd come back for sure, heavily armed and even more angry. If Sam and Roman were going to escape, it would only be by pushing forward.

25

THE WIND played with Patrick's loose curls and carried with it a definite chill. That said, the sun was out and no Irishman would ever admit to being cold when the sun was shining. He was wearing the same jeans he'd worn in Tallinn and an old Trinity College T-shirt, standing on top of the tower of St Peter's Church and looking down over Lübeck.

They hadn't got any insights from the images saved on Brett's iPad so Patrick scanned the Hanseatic buildings spread out below him, laced by the gently flowing Trave River, hoping to see some subtle clue in the city's layout. He saw nothing beyond the obvious: the glazed roofs of the Holsten Gate shone like a beacon.

The gate had been built in 1464 and was now the sole surviving piece of a much larger system of defences built before and after it. Its two conical spires, leaning lovingly towards each other, were the picturesque symbol of Lübeck and with nothing else to go on, also the most likely location for a clue.

Patrick jogged down the spiral stairway and found Brett in the church's nave, where she was rereading the brochures. 'Come, we've a gate to explore.'

They approached the gate from the city side and they could have been approaching an art gallery, its facing wall was packed with so many glass windows. The gate's martial purpose only became clear when they circled around to its outward-facing façade with its chunky walls and narrow gun slits. At least now, after centuries of conscripted service, the gate was enjoying a peaceful retirement in a flourishing riverside park.

Patrick and Brett stayed close to the walls, looking for anything that might suggest they were on the right track. The walls in question were aged red brick, bare and utilitarian but for two thin bands of decorative tiles high above their craned heads; their guidebook said they alternated randomly in groups of eight between lilies, thistles, and a lattice pattern. They'd have to take the book's word for it until they could get closer. Which is what Patrick had in mind. 'I worked in Lithuania once, with a guy who sits on the European Monuments Protection Board. I'll see if I can call in a favour and get some scaffolding put up so we can have a closer look.'

'I'm not climbing up there,' Brett said, shaking her head and stamping her left foot slowly, as if to confirm she was still on solid ground. 'We could take a peek inside in the meantime, though.'

The interior of the gate housed a small museum that was closed for pre-summer renovations, according to a sign on the door. However, like most buildings in this part of Europe, its only defence against intruders was that sign and a padlock. With two spanners and a twist, Patrick soon had the lock open.

The floor had subsided over the centuries and they had to step down as they entered the room. Someone had swept the larger brick shards into one corner and packed the unused tools near the door. The level was otherwise empty.

They stepped over a dusty velvet rope and climbed the stairs. The rear windows bathed a restored cannon in glorious sunlight, but it was the dozen model ships hanging from the ceiling that caught their attention. They were too high to study properly from there, so while Patrick fetched something to stand on, Brett searched the cannon's surface for coded messages. She didn't find anything. And when Patrick examined the ships, none was a replica of the *Drachen*.

They climbed to the next level, where the floor plan repeated, as it did on the level above and again on each of the three floors in the western tower. All were devoid of anything useful to their search so when they left the gate to look for lunch, they were tired and empty handed.

26

THE DISK in the floor was remarkable, depicting two dragons in an aerial battle above mountains whose slopes were wooded, all in exquisite detail and encrusted with jewels. Under the halogen bulbs, the dragons' scales shimmered over tensed muscles.

Sam gripped the nearest raised wing and lifted, held on, and jumped backwards. He couldn't shift it. 'Give me a hand.'

Roman grabbed the other dragon and they strained in unison. It never shifted. 'Twist?' Roman suggested.

It still didn't budge. 'This is what they went back for, I suppose, to fetch some of those explosives, no doubt.'

'So muscle isn't going to get us in, is it?' Roman completed Sam's thought. 'Not if the three of them couldn't do it.'

'No. You're right. But there must be another way.' Sam dropped onto his stomach and, with his eyes centimetres from the bright surface, ran his fingertips along its surface like he'd seen the tall man do. 'Roman, look. That's a lion there, isn't it? And a ship over there.' From the low angle he could see fine characters scratched into the surface, cleverly worked into the larger design so as to be almost invisible.

Roman dropped next to him. 'I see them. What do we do with them?'

Sam wasn't sure. Although he had precise instructions for turning the book and keys into a map, his notes had never mentioned any further barriers; the code in Tallinn had been laid out symbol by symbol and he hadn't needed to think beyond what he was given. Whoever the Nazis had gotten their information from had managed to hold a little bit back. Good on him. Sort of.

A series of clicks announced a change of state.

'What did you just do?'

'I pressed in this sheep, here.'

Sam saw that the sheep symbol was indented, although the clicking had stopped now. Nothing else had happened.

'Should I try another one?'

Sam shrugged, and Roman pressed in the lion.

There was another short burst of noise and the lion stayed depressed. And still nothing happened. And still the disk wouldn't move. When Roman pressed in the ship, it stayed depressed for a second, and then all three symbols popped back up, their fit so precise that it was no longer possible to see the seams. Roman continued to press characters at random. Each time, after the third or fourth one, the buttons popped back up.

Sam peered over Roman's shoulder. 'It's a combination lock, something like the one in Tallinn, I should guess.'

'Ah, Sam, those other guys, you remember them, the ones with more guns than we have; yeah, well, they don't want to find us in here stealing what they perceive to be their treasure, so if you've seen this all before, why don't we just do the same thing here instead of pissing about playing pokey-pokey?'

'It's not quite the same. It was written in the book then, literally step by step. I have no instructions this time around, except that I can see that it uses the same symbols. . . .'

Sam had skimmed through the book he had taken from Brett, thinking that he needed it only for the maps it had encoded in its illuminated script, but along with each map there was a fairy tale, the sort you'd find in a children's book. He had read the story about Riga on the bus, but at the time he had dismissed it as a clever veil, camouflage, because who would take a collection of fairy tales seriously?

Well, he did now.

Sam grabbed the book and paged to the story he remembered.

'Roman, listen to this: *The sheep had come down with a strange malady: though they ate as much as ever, they grew thin and withered, and then died without exception. In fact, sheep were dying in large numbers all across Latvia. Everyone was affected, except for one farmer. His flock was spared; not even a single lamb was lost. To the villagers, this was sufficient proof of witchcraft and they had him thrown in jail.*

'*It was on the day of his public arrest that the* Drachen *happened to dock in Riga to stock up on provisions. The captain, seeing the mob and fearing for the farmer's safety, offered his services as a neutral outsider to defend the man in court. . . .*'

The disk was whirring and clicking again; and the sheep and the ship characters were depressed.

'I thought I'd go along with the story.'

'Carry on. I hope you're right. *The farmer protested his innocence, though he could give no reason for his sheep being spared: he said they drank from the same river and grazed on the same slopes as the other sheep; the only difference was that they always slept in his field. But everyone's sheep always slept in their owners' fields. The mob was calling for the farmer's head.*

'The captain appealed for calm and asked to be allowed to visit the field in question. Though the villagers were against the idea, the captain persisted until they relented.

'The captain felt a chill as they approached the field. The horses became agitated and refused to go beyond the circle of stones that formed its border. The men dismounted and walked the last hundred paces, most now clutching crucifixes to their chests.

'For all that, it was an ordinary field, except that it was round and had a three metre high mound at its centre. The captain ordered the farmer to dig there. As he did, a shining sword was revealed. . . .'

Sam could hear shouting now, and thundering boots. Sam looked at the disk; it was still clicking but not yet open. He skimmed the rest of the passage, 'It was a dragon's sword. If there's a dragon, push it in. Um, yada, yada, yada, then he threw it in the well, is there a well? And all the animals got better and the farmer was released. Nice, a happy ending. Have you got that well, yet?'

'No, I can't find it.' Roman's gaze was bouncing back and forth across the disk.

'There will be one, keep looking.'

'There had better be, because this disk isn't moving.'

A torch beam flickered in. 'Keep looking, keep looking.'

The first man that burst into the chamber was short and burly. Sam fired two quick shots. Neither hit him. But they did force him back. Sam reloaded. Roman was sweating under the lights, his eyes still locked on the disk.

A volley of shots scattered into the room and Sam fired twice more. The clicking stopped as he reloaded. 'Got it!' Roman shouted.

Sam fired again. Then the whirring stopped, too. Sam fired again. Roman cursed. Sam reloaded and fired again. The characters remained depressed. Nothing else happened. Sam fired again and reloaded.

The disk popped up, and Roman dragged it aside as two streams of bullets punched through the room – one coming high and one coming low. Sam emptied both chambers, slid the last two cartridges home, fired again, and followed Roman, pulling the disk closed as he dropped into the shaft below.

27

'DAMN IT, Englishman, I'm on your side.' Sam's fall had been broken by Roman, who wasn't happy about his role. But both men had escaped any serious injury. They dusted themselves off and switched on their headlamps as above them, heavy cutting tools were already whining to life.

The cylindrical shaft they were standing in barely stretched past their fingertips, but for such a small space, it hid its exit well. Roman was the one to find it – like an upside-down post box, it was cut by a low and rectangular opening at shin height – and he dived right in.

Sam slung the duffle bag over his shoulder, and chased the scrape and squelch of Roman down the tunnel; his headlamp had taken a knock in the fall and the loose bulb's bouncing light liquefied his surroundings to the point that he was battling nausea as he raced to catch up.

Roman's hands finally found open space. He gave a final push and was vomited from the tunnel. He wiped a thick sludge of sweat and grit from his forehead and took a seat, sticky and exhausted, on the cool floor. Black and white hexagons, under centuries of dust, tiled the floor, not side by side like on a soccer ball but in larger patches of light and shadow. The reach of his headlamp revealed no more. Though eager to explore, he sat there, breathing heavily, waiting for Sam to catch up.

It was like a clearing in a stone forest. Arboreal pillars grew at irregular intervals throughout the space. Their trunks, painstakingly carved to mimic the texture of tree bark, supported a canopy of high branches from which the remnants of chandeliers still hung. Even the floor was an artwork; scattered among the black and white tiles were ones carved into shallow patches of wild flowers, delicate in their details but robust enough to be walked on. The surreal grand hall was dominated by a raw wood banquet table; thirty high-back chairs flanked its length, all deferring to a throne that presided from a raised platform at the table's head. While the chairs were empty, a single armour-clad skeleton occupied this place of honour, its flesh and clothes having long since dissolved into history.

Sam approached their host and picked up his sword. It had a comforting weight, was well balanced and swift through the air, and free of flamboyant decorations – a soldier's weapon, not a ceremonial prop. But also not a clue.

After five minutes, Sam's clear footprints marked his patrol around the table but he had nothing else to show for his efforts. 'You got anything on your side, big guy?'

'Nothing here.'

The sanctity of the dead could no longer be preserved.

Sam stripped the old bones of their armour. The skeleton was an empty cage. That is what he expected of course, though still he had hoped to find the next dragon hidden there, perhaps where the heart used to be. He picked up the helmet and turned it in his hands. It was heavy, made from forged steel, studded by a single black stone and trimmed by a thin silver band that ran along its edges, mimicking the pattern of the armour's chest piece. He examined that next. There was nothing of interest there either.

Except ... as Sam placed the chest plate on the table, he noticed a line of engraved script. Though it was written in an obscure German dialect, Sam recognised it: Luke 14, verse 10.

But, when thou be called, recline in the lowest place, that he who called thee may say to thee, friend, come up higher; then thou shalt have glory before those reclining with thee.

28

WHILE SAM was searching the main hall, Roman searched the rear where an avenue of the carved pillars created an annex that might once have been a staging area for grand banquets. It was empty now, except, he hoped, for a clue.

The floor was scuffed and plain black, the walls smoke-stained but bare; that left the pillars. Abstract patterns had been carved into their inward-facing surfaces like lovers' graffiti. He stared and circled them as an old memory teased him.

'What are you doing?' Roman asked.

Sam had pushed the table aside and was hammering the tiles with the back of a sword. 'There was an inscription in the armour and I'm sure the dragon is hidden below the foot of this table.'

'What sort of inscription?'

'A Bible verse.'

Roman raised an eyebrow.

'I know,' Sam said. 'But have you found anything?'

'Good point. You run with that.' Roman watched Sam toil, but each blow of the sword was like the tick of a clock and he was getting fidgety; he needed to do something. 'Hey, Sam, watch this.'

'What the hell are you doing?'

Roman was grinning. He had lifted one of the chairs above his head and then he smashed it into the floor. The reverberation shook his arms but the chair held its form. 'Ah. Well, it was meant to break first time.'

'That's the one part I understood. Would you care to explain the "why"?'

'Watch and learn, buddy, watch and learn.'

The chair lasted two further blows, then the cross-strut broke and after that it went to pieces. Sam shook his head and returned to his own destructive actions while Roman broke down three more chairs.

Roman ferried the wooden fragments into the tunnel, disappearing for a minute with each load. As he exited the tunnel for the fourth time, he dusted off his hands, rummaged in his pocket, and lit a cigarette. 'Fancy a drag?'

'No, my wife would kill me. What are you doing, though? We don't have time for relaxing.'

Roman shook his head and took another lazy drag, then crawled back into the tunnel. He touched the orange tip of the cigarette to a pile of splinters and blew softly, nurturing the flame until the old kindling caught alight.

A minute later, acrid smoke followed him back into the grand hall.

'There are already people out there who are trying to kill us, I don't need you to help them.'

'Says the man who, not twenty minutes ago, dived right onto my head.'

'Touché.'

'I didn't have to go to Sandhurst to be taught the value of a defensive barrier. Why don't you keep on doing the manual labour there, and I'll apply my superior intellect to finding us a way out?'

Roman dodged the piece of tile that Sam tossed at him and scampered to the back of the hall. Something about those pillars was still nagging at him.

Kalev's men had cut open the bronze disk but this wasn't a time for celebrating, it was a time for decisive action. He watched the two men clip themselves to a nylon climbing rope and abseil into the darkness, then he swung a kit bag onto his back and followed them down, already barking orders to lift the pace.

After twenty minutes of steady slog, he bumped into the boots of the man in front of him. 'Keep going!'

'I can't sir, sorry, sir.' Shouts were relayed forward and back like five-year-olds playing a party game. 'He says there's a fire blocking the tunnel; says he can't proceed.'

'Tell him to clear it, he has two minutes.'

29

B URNING COALS flew into the room like uncontained pop-
corn. Roman's barricade was being shot to pieces, but for
the moment, the danger was being funnelled into a single,
bullet-infested channel. Crouched alongside the firing line,
Sam knew that even that relative safety wouldn't last. What had
they missed? The thin outline of a door? The slight rise of a
bricked-over blasting cap? A subtle dragon symbol? His eyes
moved fast, too fast he knew, but it was hard to stay calm amid
the noise and chaos. 'Roman? Where's that way out? Roman!'

All the while bullets were turning the table into a cloud of
splinters, a fact he only noticed when a maroon package broke
into view *inside* the foot of the table. He stared for a second –
damn the Germans and their pedantic wording. The next
dragon was mere metres away.

Unfortunately, those metres were guarded by a continuous
patrol of bullets.

And then the bullets stopped.

No one could hear Kalev's yelling anymore. They either had
their fingers stuffed into their ears, like he did, or they had been
deafened by the explosion of automatic gunfire.

It took two minutes for the shrill tinnitus to subside in its wake. 'Update.'

Kalev's command started a chain reaction.

'Fires out. Coals have been cleared. We can go.'

'Then why aren't we already going? Go, go, go.'

Sam took a breath, acknowledged that what he was about to do was stupid, and then did it. He sprinted to the table, collecting the sword en route, and hacked away at the lace of wood that held his prize. It took four solid strikes to cut it free. Sam grabbed the wrapped bundle and squeezed the hard sphere inside; its felt whole. Thank God. He turned and sprinted back out of harm's way.

'Freeze!'

Sam turned, keeping a tight grip on the package. The two men flanking Kalev had their guns trained on Sam.

'Put it down.'

Roman was studying the pillars in the back room, again. Something about them bothered him. Each was wrapped in patterns that looked different, but felt related.

Then the shots came.

Roman rushed to help Sam, then stopped. He could be an unarmed friend in a gunfight, or he could take a risk that might free them both. Sam would understand.

Roman had caught the image from the perfect angle. The pillars were like a sculpture of the last supper he had once seen alongside the River Weir in Durham. Those had been a masterpiece by Colin Wilburn carved into twelve reclaimed elm trunks: fragmented placement and cunning design working together so that what appeared chaotic snapped into a three-dimensional picture when viewed from a single perfect spot. He didn't know who had carved these pillars, but the concept was the same.

Roman took a step left, watched as the scene faded away, took a step right and watched it reappear. Only a small portion of each pillar's engravings was relevant, the rest was seamless camouflage. The picture depicted the grand hall as it must once have been: rugs covered the floor and tapestries the walls, a knight sat feasting in each chair, while a large dragon slept on the floor as peacefully as a well-fed dog.

The carving was ingenious, but it didn't appear to mean anything.

Roman blocked out the sound of shooting and stared.

Peeking out from under the nose of the sleeping dragon was a key. The shooting stopped and Roman knew he didn't have time to doubt his gut. He sprinted into the other room, just as someone yelled 'Freeze'.

30

'TAKE YOUR gun out, slowly, and drop it on the floor.'
   'I'm unarmed, the only gun is over there.' Sam nodded
his head towards the shattered table.
   'Lift up your shirt and turn around.'
   Sam complied.
   'Tell your friend, wherever he is hiding, to come out with his
hands in the air.'
   'He's already gone.'
   Kalev applied visible pressure to the trigger.
   'It's true. But it doesn't matter, you don't need him.'
   'Hand over the dragon and I'll accept that logic.'
   'Just one is no good to you, you need them all.'
   'Give me that dragon now, and shut up. I'll take the others
from you in a minute.'
   Sam unwrapped the package and placed the amber globe on
the table; a flick of his wrist was enough to roll it just out of
reach. Now the beanpole in his ridiculous suit couldn't order
him to hand it over without also giving him an opportunity to
turn his back, move his hands, and possibly launch a counter
attack. Not that Sam knew what he would do with such an
opportunity.

'Now the others.'

'I don't have them, not here with me.'

'Where are they?'

'They're in Tallinn.'

'We'll soon find out. Sit on the floor with your hands on your head.' Kalev inclined his head and one of his men marched forward and grabbed the ripped duffle bag.

Roman chose to ignore the instruction he heard in Sam's protest. He wouldn't leave a friend behind to be executed and he was under no illusions about Kalev's ultimate play. His eyes darted back and forth as he crept through the stone forest, between triangulating the implied location of the sleeping dragon and looking at Sam, who was sitting on the floor ten metres away.

Sam was right: Roman never had a plan of attack. Instead he had a long wish list of things that needed to go right: he needed to find the right spot, he needed to reach that spot before being shot, he needed the mechanism to still be functional after 700 years, and, of course, he needed to get himself and Sam safely through whatever door it opened, again before being shot. He just needed all the luck in the world.

Sam knew that in a few seconds the two amber globes would be found; and he was certain that, when they were, he would be killed. So he played his last card. 'How did you find this place? I thought I was the only one who knew the code.'

The man ignored him.

'Did you follow me? Think about it. Because how are you going to find the next dragon if I'm not there?'

Sam made eye contact with the leader, ignoring the acolyte behind him rifling through the bag.

'You're a fool. Killing me will doom you to losing the treasure.'

The man bit his ruler-straight lower lip in an uncomfortably boyish gesture. 'I'm no fool. You'll have told me everything by the time you die.'

His lieutenant coughed discreetly and lifted the remaining globes, but dropped them again when running footsteps burst to life. All three soldiers started firing in scribbled figures of eight.

Roman took three more steps and dived to the floor, sliding on his belly with his left hand reaching in front of him.

31

B RETT AND Patrick were sitting outside a cafe on Lübeck's
town square. Their now well-thumbed guidebook had
recommended it for its impressive selection of German lunch
meats; they had sat down when they saw its dewed flotilla of
beer taps. It had been that sort of a day. Of course, the patterned
tiles on the Holsten Gate still had the potential to hide a clue,
but any clue they had missed would be impossible to interpret
without the book that Sam had stolen. The weather was good,
though. Patrick raised his glass and appreciated the perfectly
poured lager the way a jeweller might appreciate a brilliant
diamond.

When he looked up, he could sense that Brett was less
content. 'What's wrong?'

To an observer, they were just another spring couple, but
although Brett kept her face demurely downturned, her eyes
were flicking urgently. Patrick stretched his eyes as far around
as they would go. Brett nodded. Whatever it was was right
behind him.

Patrick picked up a polished salt shaker, tapped some salt
onto his open-faced sandwich, and replaced it; he had seen the
warped reflection of two men. Brett reached into her bag and

fished out a pen and postcard. *Those men were part of the team that stole the* Drachen *from me.*

Patrick read the note, scribbled a response, and passed it back.

She read it and scowled. Brett was nervous and Patrick could understand why. But he had to take advantage of the fact that he wasn't known to these men by following them, even if that meant she would be alone at the hotel. She would be safe there. And it wouldn't be for long.

Brett scribbled some notes and slid the postcard back to Patrick. He looked up and shrugged; it wasn't the first time he'd misread a woman. Brett had crossed out the section about her returning to the hotel and replaced it with the words 'hides and watches'. She wasn't going to sit on the sidelines.

'Fine, Sweetie.' He laughed at her reaction to that. Although Brett's involvement made his task more complicated, this wasn't a fight he was going to win by arguing: she would leave first, melt into the crowd, and find a suitable forward observation post; Patrick would stay behind and wait for the men to finish their meal. And if he was lucky, another drink.

32

FROM WHAT Patrick could hear of their conversation, these men were simple employees; still, they might lead him to someone more useful. When they signalled for their bill, Patrick dropped some notes onto the table and followed a few paces behind them.

Three minutes later, Patrick stepped out of a doorway and joined the throng of tourists meandering through the Old Town, a little jealous that he couldn't share their leisure. The two men were a few paces in front now, and looking unconcerned. He noticed Brett leave her post when they passed – typical – and she was now a similar distance behind.

Patrick picked up his pace and as soon as he got a chance, ducked left into a side street and started to run. He dashed between eclectic storefronts, turning left again at the first cross street, and he kept running, all the way back to the main street. There he stopped and looked quickly back down the alley: Brett was nowhere to be seen. Good. He had known she'd take the bait. It was for the best. She'd be catching up soon, though.

Patrick barged through the crowd to make up his lost ground. Maybe his detour had been a mistake; the two heads he was supposed to be following were shrinking quickly and he was still being slowed by the idle human traffic. And then they were gone. Patrick broke into a full sprint, his curls whipping up around him in the breeze. There was only one road they could have taken, but after that. . . .

As Patrick rounded the corner, he saw them rounding the next. He ran to that corner and stopped.

The street ahead was empty. Up ahead a small fountain was the hub around which four streets spoked out; all of them were empty and all the buildings that lined them were multi-storey residential units. There were a thousand places the men could have gone.

Patrick shrugged and ran right, following a hunch since he had nothing else to follow.

When that ended in another impossible choice between empty streets, he gave up and headed back to the hotel, wondering if there was anything he could say that might placate Brett. He'd buy her a bottle of tequila on the way; if that didn't work, nothing would.

Brett watched Patrick spin around at the fountain and head off in the wrong direction. She thought of calling out to him, but she was fed up with being mollycoddled. He had tried to keep her out of this twice now and if he knew she was still around, he would do it again.

Anyway, Patrick's theatrics offered an opportunity which she'd be foolish to spurn. From the way the men had increased their speed in town, she was sure they knew they were being followed. With any luck, seeing Patrick make his flustered wrong turns would have put them at ease. The coast was clear and now it was her turn.

33

S AM LAUNCHED himself at the approaching soldier. His stiff elbow caught the man square on the chin and both men crashed to the floor. When Sam rose, it was with the soldier's gun in his hands. But he didn't get a chance to use it before he had to dive behind a pillar, which a volley of shots was already turning to pumice stone.

Sam swung the gun up to his shoulder and returned fire.

Roman slid across the floor. He was aiming for the one flower that looked a shade less black than its neighbours, and praying.

His fingers felt cool bronze and he pulled it.

Kalev heard a loud crack to his left and concentrated his fire there.

The diversion was a fickle ally, drawing fire away from Roman but directing it towards his intended destination. Oh well. Roman pushed himself up into a crouched run and zigzagged towards the door that had opened in the wall.

Sam heard a crack and felt a puff of air. Roman must have opened an exit. Good for him. Hopefully he could make a dash for safety. It was too late for Sam though; even armed with the unconscious soldier's gun, he'd never get past the two men still standing. That didn't mean he was out of options, though.

Sam fired two wild bursts, then sprinted for the smoke-stained tunnel that had brought them all there. He dived in without looking, chased by a squadron of fresh bullets.

Roman sprinted for the door, a trail of bullet-shattered tiles in his wake.

Kalev cursed at the ceiling, then shouted a string of precise orders: the standing man checked his weapons, checked his torch, checked his downed colleague, slapped him awake, stripped him of his extra ammunition, tossed one of the magazines to Kalev, pocketed another, and then chased Sam down the tunnel. With more men stationed in the church, Kalev saw no reason to over-commit resources to that particular hunt.

Instead Kalev carried out the same equipment checks and followed Roman through the door that had sprung open in the wall. His prey had a head start.

With long strides, he started to run downhill. The tunnel was like a square corkscrew, digging deep below the church. Kalev was catching glimpses of the fleeing man now.

Sam reached the access shaft and rejoiced in the opportunity to stretch his back and neck. A climbing rope still hung into the well. Rigged? He gave it a tug and jumped back. Nothing happened. That didn't mean that no one was waiting above, of course, watching it like an Inuit fisherman on an ice shelf, but he had no choice; he had to risk the climb.

He broke the surface with a quick gopher peek. The room above was empty. Sam climbed out, pulled up the rope, pushed the heavy disk closed, and looked around the chamber. It was as they'd left it, though now only one lamp burned. At least they were eco-friendly assassins.

He got moving. He might have solved one of his problems, but he hadn't solved them all.

Roman was exhausted and in pain, grazed by several of the bullets that had been haphazardly sent his way and bruised from the dive. He promised his body that each next turn would be the last, but the tunnel never ended, and his pursuer never slowed. Then he skidded around a corner into a wide T-junction against a solid wall. He ran forwards, looking for a door. There had to be a door. Maybe to the left. Or to the right. He couldn't see a door yet. But it was dark. Maybe it was to the left. As his eyes strained he missed a step, his front foot dropped, and his momentum bowled him along the floor. His dropped torch clattered ahead then died.

The pain that bolted from his ankle reduced his top speed to a hobble and there was still no door. He rubbed the wall as if he might find Braille instructions on its rough surface. His heart pounded in his chest. Approaching footsteps pounded in his ears.

34

BRETT HAD crept through a row of small front gardens, keeping to the shadows, and now she was crouched behind a dark blue panel van parked in front of the building that the men had disappeared into.

She took a moment to check the front windows. Nothing moved, so she scrambled into the driveway and sprinted to where a wooden gate barred access to a communal utility space. Brett clambered over the gate and found herself among wet washing and old rubbish.

Two cellar doors lead into the building, but both were locked. She could enter via one of the frosted bathroom windows that looked down on her from each floor, since many of them stood open.

Brett paused and weighed up her options. Only one of the six washing lines was occupied; the bright sunshine would surely lure out more housewives before long so that would be her plan A; but if no one came out soon she would climb.

Fifteen minutes later, the door bumped open, followed by the plump rear end of a woman burdened with two armfuls of wet laundry. Brett hadn't wanted to wait too close to the stinking rubbish bins and had barely reached cover in time. Now, she wondered if hiding so far away hadn't been a mistake. She tensed as the door swung closed.

It stopped short. The woman had used a half-brick as a doorstop and the moment she bent down, Brett took her chance.

The hinges squeaked as Brett pulled the door fully open, but by then she was inside. Inside being a musty laundry room; two machines were spinning loads while four more stood empty. She moved past them to a service stairway. Yellow paint flaked off the walls and the wooden steps creaked with each step.

A corridor of shabby back doors ran the length of each floor. Brett climbed to the fifth floor. If her estimate was right, her target was the fourth flat along but she paused to listen at each door she passed, just in case. The first three were silent. At the fourth she heard male voices. They were faint, though, so she leaned in.

And then the door flew inwards, followed by Brett.

35

KALEV SAW Roman immediately, silhouetted in the beam of his torch like the titles of a James Bond movie; so much so, that the splash of blood after he shot him tipped the scene towards cliché.

Pain hijacked Roman's senses. Instantly omnipresent, it gradually migrated towards the wound in his right arm where it settled, and throbbed, and multiplied. With each slowing heartbeat, more of his blood pumped onto the floor.

Kalev finally had some good news to report. He took out his phone to call Hiko, but so far underground there was no signal.

It was probably better to wait until he could confirm both deaths, anyway. Nevertheless, Hiko wouldn't pay without photographic evidence so, with his phone still out, Kalev walked towards the corpse.

The bolted foot of a ladder poked into the bubble of dim light in which Roman lay, climbing down from somewhere . . . anywhere, it didn't actually matter. Though now he could see that it wasn't a single, coincidental ladder, but rather a series of ladders that extended as wide as his field of vision.

Roman forced the swirling picture into focus. Obviously he was supposed to know which ladder to choose. Still, it didn't really matter, any port in a storm. Roman exploded upwards, moving from lying to crouching to jumping in a fraction of a second; his left hand opened and stretched upwards in hope.

Kalev's phone was still dropping when he fired the first shot.

Roman grabbed the ladder's lowest rung, roaring against the pain that almost threw him off. He hooked his left elbow around the second rung and swung his legs up as a bullet punctured the wall below him.

He had actually been quite a good climber once, most special forces soldiers were, but the years since had included quite a few idle hours and even more late nights; he still stayed in shape, but these days he gymed to get big, not to get strong, and he was carrying an injury. Still, to fall now was to die, of that he was sure, so he gritted his teeth and ascended as quickly as he could.

Kalev fired upwards in frustration. Bullets clattered off the rows of ladders that ran up the wall all around him. He fired a second angry burst and when no body fell, he started to climb.

As his eyes adjusted to the dark, Roman began to see that the other ladders were similar, but not the same; as he continued upwards, the ladder immediately to his right stopped short; and then the one immediately to his left did too. So that's how it worked. He had no way of knowing if he was climbing towards freedom or just towards a slightly higher dead end.

The ladder went suddenly still. The man he was after must have reached the top. Kalev took out his torch and probed the gloom with its fading beam. Then he heard movement to his left. He fired three times and waited. Fired again and waited. Still there was no falling body, so he reloaded and resumed his climb.

The scanning torch beam had reflected off a ladder far to his left and Roman began the traverse. His hands were sweating and his arm was on fire. And then the shooting started. And stopped. And started and stopped.

Kalev reached the top of the ladder. There was no door. No landing. No destination whatsoever. He was still going to get his man, this just complicated matters slightly.

Roman felt the ladder tremble under the weight of a second climber. Already? And then the fringes of a torch beam stretched upwards again, seeking him out. Roman pressed himself flat against the wall and hoped for the best. Locked in that intimate embrace with the ladder, he finally saw its code.

He started climbing as soon as the beam died.

A minute later he crawled onto a narrow walkway that ran the full width of the wall, providing access to a fresh series of twelve ladders. Roman paused briefly at each ladder as he jogged past it, and selected the third.

Kalev pulled himself onto the walkway. He stood there for a beat, flicking the light left and right, enjoying having something dependable to stand on; then he walked right, found the ladder, and started to climb.

As Roman climbed, he saw the ladders on either side of him terminate early while his continued up. He had cracked the code; though the ladder sagged once again, too soon. The lanky bastard had followed him and Roman thought he knew how: he'd been leaving a trail of bloody handprints like road signs.

Roman hopped onto a second landing and started to run, passing six ladders before he found the one marked with a sword. He moved two ladders back and started to climb. After ten steps, Roman drew the knife from his ankle sheath, rapped it on the ladder, and leant out until a shot hit close by.

After two quick breaths, Roman was climbing again.

When Roman could see the ladder's end approaching, he stopped and waited as blood pooled in his hand then made a crimson splash to his right, tucked his wounded hand into his armpit, and started a one-handed and probably ill-advised climb to the left.

The ladder was abruptly short and empty. A trail of blood went off to the right – what, did he think that Kalev was afraid to climb? Kalev wasn't, but he would prefer not to. He unholstered his gun and fired a wide fan of shots to his right. He reloaded and fired a second arc. Then he reloaded and did the same to his left; it paid to be thorough.

By the time Kalev heard the crack, it was too late. Above him and to his left a flash of light outlined a door opening in the wall. He emptied his clip at it, and then the door was pulled closed again.

36

S AM STALKED through the tunnel, stopping at the last corner where light from the church washed in. The outline of a guard receded and returned, receded and returned, every thirty seconds, and the voices coming from the church's interior spoke of more in reserve. His plan wouldn't work.

But what the hell? Roman never had a plan, after all.

Sam took aim and fired and the guard pirouetted to the ground, dead. Then the next dropped on the threshold. Now the others were warned. Sam fired a few more shots to keep them back, spun, and ran back down the tunnel. He skidded into the room and, despite the beat of approaching boots, he risked a moment on his stomach with his back to the door.

Sam tapped in the code, hefted the disk to the side, dropped the climbing rope back into position, and killed the lights. Only to switch them back on a second later as the first guard entered the room, blinking at the wall of light. The following man collided with him, and Sam shot them both. Sam killed the lights again, leant forward and fired into the well, turned back and fired as more guards tried to storm the chamber, fired a final burst into the well, and then rolled into a corner.

Bullets entered the room from both sides. Sam turned on the lights as four men barrelled into the room, heading straight for the well. The first one there gripped the rope with a gloved hand and led them down with his gun firing on full automatic. Two more followed him with their weapons drawn but quiet. The last man stepped back from the well and looked around. When he shouted a question to his colleagues below, Sam's hand was forced.

Sam ran low. The man turned towards the sound as Sam crashed into his weight-bearing knee. A stream of bullets arced up the wall, and along the ceiling as the guard tumbled backwards into the well.

Sam cut the climbing rope, slammed the disk closed, and sprinted down the passage, his gun raised and ready.

The church appeared empty. Sam wasn't taking any chances, though. He stayed close to the wall, kept his finger inside the trigger guard, and moved warily, resisting the urge to run towards the front door and the sunshine he knew was beyond it. Fortunately so, because just metres from freedom he heard footfall.

Sam broke the embrace first and stepped back. Roman wore an uneven grin, but his skin was cold to the touch and white; and a second later, he collapsed to his haunches. Sam put an arm around his friend and helped him out of the church, as Roman's blood stained both their shirts.

37

'WHAT IS the nature of your emergency?'
'There've been gunshots at St John's church. Send the police!'

'Certainly, sir. Can I—'

But the line was already dead, the phone already binned. Kalev had smelt the remnants of a contained gunfight, stepped over the bodies, and made good his escape. The police would arrive too late for the priest or his fallen men, but that was of little concern to him, they would tidy up his mess and stop anyone else from following his trail. Taxpayer money well spent, in his opinion.

Kalev's other phone started to ring a second later.

'Sir.'

'You have retrieved the dragons.'

'No, not yet.'

Hiko paused. 'I hired you because you said that you were, and I quote, "a real soldier, not a soft officer who has only ever read about fighting in a book". So far, you are not living up to that boast. I gave you an opportunity, to pay back my advance and walk away. I am not the sort of man that makes an offer twice, so whether I hired badly or you performed badly is now irrelevant. I will hold you to our agreement.'

'Yes, sir. We are making progress, though, sir. We have captured the woman and I am going to Lübeck now to question her.'

'No. I'll speak to her. Just make sure she is secure. Find her hotel and have it searched. And then call me back.'

Kalev swore once more and pocketed the silent device. He was an orderly man, a man who spent a great deal of his time and resources ensuring his environment conformed to his needs, but today he found himself surrounded by chaos. Hiko was right to be angry. He was angry himself. That woman was a curse. It was all her fault. This was no longer about money, it was about professional pride.

Hiko looked up when the bell chimed. The middle-aged Chinese man that had just walked into Hin Ho Curry House went by the name of Wilsin, though that was certainly an alias.

Wilsin was shorter than Hiko, and wiry, with an air about him that suggested he was unlikely to be beaten in a fair fight and even less likely to ever fight fair. Hiko put his phone away and waved him over.

Typically, Hiko would send an emissary to handle these interactions. Or, if he was forced to do it personally, he would pretend to be that lowly worker. But Hiko didn't like Wilsin's patronising sneer, so he tossed him a roll of bank notes and got straight down to business.

'I need to arrange a hit. Untraceable. They must bring their own guns.'

'Will they encounter resistance?'

'Probably.'

He measured the notes between his fingers. 'Triads?'

'Not triads. No affiliations.'

'Disposable, you mean?' There was no hint of judgment in the question.

'Yes.'

'There are a couple of Mainland kids who go around Mong Kok pretending to be triads. The real-deal think they're a joke, so they're desperate for an opportunity to make a mark. These kids learned everything they know from Cantonese action movies so they'll be noisy, but they're not professionals so they'll need a two-on-one advantage.'

'Cheap?'

Wilsin had a great poker face. He put the money in his shirt pocket. 'This will do for now. The same again on completion.'

'Fine.'

'Who's the target?'

'In here.' Hiko tapped a manila envelope and slid it across the table. 'Tell them to watch that address until I give the signal. Then they must kill the target immediately. And there's no need to be subtle about it.'

Wilsin gave him a curt nod.

'And I have one more job for you, I need some information.'

38

SAM HAD applied basic first aid before driving Roman to a neighbourhood doctor, one who didn't believe in any paperwork beyond that minted by the US government. He was now sitting alone, waiting for the pretty nurse to report back on the surgery. The old book he'd taken from Brett was open in his lap and he flipped through it.

Five minutes later, he closed it again. There was no way to guess the next location.

What he needed to know for sure was if Roman had seen any numbers during his escape. Roman had been so proud of himself on the drive over, regularly answering Sam's question with a big smile and a number. Unfortunately, the number he claimed to remember was different with each retelling. Some of those numbers corresponded to cities in the book, but most didn't. Sam had to hope he'd remember more clearly with fresh blood and generic painkillers flowing through his system.

Sam picked up a tattered copy of *National Geographic,* the sole English magazine in the room, and paged through a story on rhino poaching. Bastards.

He slapped the magazine closed and jumped up – if Roman had seen the number, known it was important, then maybe he had taken a photo. Sam went to the counter where Roman's belongings had been left; among them was an iPhone. Sam found the picture easily: it looked like a plaque commemorating the laying of a keystone – a sleeping dragon flanked by an eleven and a twenty-three. Sam opened the book again and turned to page eleven. He was going to Gdansk, Poland.

The nurse explained Roman's drug regime and handed Sam two bottles of pills. He pocketed them and handled the payment before leading Roman to the car.

'So, where are we going next?' Roman asked.

'Home for some R&R.'

'I mean, *where are we going next?*' Roman asked again, seemingly feeling better already.

'Are you up for another challenge?'

'Always.'

'Great. The doctor said you should take four pain pills with food, so let's have lunch and then I'll explain everything. Did he do a good job, by the way?'

'Yeah, I think so. Better than the army butchers, that's for sure.' Roman stretched and flexed his arm to test it out.

Back at the apartment, Sam put two frozen pizzas in the oven and handed Roman a glass of water and four tablets. 'So, do you remember that number you saw in the church?'

Roman didn't answer. He was already asleep.

Sam left a pizza out for Roman, wolfed down the other, and then called a taxi.

39

THEY HAD been so clever hiding it with all that gold. People haven't changed. They always were and always are, looking for gold. Jaume Ferrer was looking for gold. Jaime Ferrer was looking for gold. The girl and her friends were looking for gold. But not Hiko. Everyone else asked *where* the treasure was. He asked *what* the treasure was. And that would make the difference.

The legend talked about a treasure that would change the course of the war. And the legend had mentioned gold. So the world put two and two together and imagined a hoard big enough to fund a standing army. The world looked for sparkle and they would find it. Hiko was looking for something else. He would find that, too.

What Jaume and Jaime Ferrer had never understood was that the elders were not seeking to protect what they knew from the villagers, they were seeking to protect the villagers from what they knew: the gold that now filled the chamber was guarded by a very real, very deadly dragon.

Unknown years earlier, a young boy digging a well on the dry highlands had broken into a series of subterranean tunnels.

Although they were dry, the tunnels echoed with the sound of flowing water. He followed the sound, hoping the acrid stench that grew with each step didn't mean the spring had been fouled.

Thirty minutes later, he found a cavern with a pool and the source of the smell. A teal blue mould had turned the walls furry, covering every surface — floor, walls, and ceiling — in its drooping tendrils. The boy paused and dragged a tentative finger across the closest wall. It came away covered in blue dust. He rubbed the sample between his thumb and forefinger, invoking a vinegar scent. Then he touched it to his tongue. As dry as his mouth was, he spat it out as the bitter taste drew bile from his empty stomach.

The boy walked towards the pool and knelt at its edge. With the taste of the mould still burning his mouth, he took a tentative sip. The water was cold, sweet and pure. He drank heartily and filled his gourds. Then he dived in, washing the baked desert dust from his tired body.

He stayed in the cave for an hour, swimming and napping, until he decided to carry his good news home. As he jogged out of the strange cavern, he paused at the tunnel entrance and took a final deep breath, then ran laughing towards home.

As he ran, his mood turned more serious, and by the time he walked into his village, he was sullen.

The boy told no one of his find. He wasn't sure why. Water was the lifeblood of every desert community and a new spring was a treasure, but he already knew that it was going to be his secret.

The next day he returned, bringing incense to counter the mould's aroma.

And he returned daily for a fortnight. Willingly, at first, but then because he had to quench the fire that burned in his throat. Eventually every minute he wasn't in the cavern was an unbearable hell; and by then, he could barely walk, so he spilled his secret.

When inhaled, the mould spores took root in the mucus membrane of the nasal passages, producing a subtle euphoria that swelled as the colony spread. After a week, the host would be feeling happier and fitter than he had ever felt in his life. After another week, he'd be overwhelmed by the mental and physical need for more. And just a week after that, he'd be dead.

Addiction tore through the thatch-roof village without mercy, claiming two out of every three villagers as its own, with little regard for age or status. Even the few whose lucky genes somehow rendered them immune felt its fiery breath, as the crazed addicts turned on everyone else.

To end the terror, the untouched had to make the brutal decision to euthanise the stricken.

Finally only six villagers were left alive.

One of the survivors realised the cave could be their salvation. Its location became their most sacred secret; but even if it was ever discovered by a thief, the mould was a lethal guarantee of security. And there was a big demand for that sort of security, removed as it was from the king's watchful eyes.

As word spread of the strongbox in the desert, the stockpile of gold under their stewardship grew, until, a generation later, the offspring of those guilt-burdened villagers had become the de facto bankers of Mali's underworld. Until the king found out.

The youngest of the tribesman, perhaps slighted by some insult, but probably motivated by pure greed, had sought out an audience with the royal advisors.

He told them of the untaxed wealth, he showed them the tribe's ledgers, and, having stoked their ire, he suggested the tribe be made an example of. What he didn't tell them, was that the gold wasn't actually in the village. And by the time the king's assassins returned *blood-soaked but empty handed, he had disappeared again. Now only one man in the world knew the cave's location.*

Hiko wanted that blue dragon. He wanted, more than anything, the chaos it would bring.

When the younger Ferrer returned to Europe with the stolen gold, some of the mould would almost certainly have accompanied him. Hiko only needed a few spores.

Two large monitors sat side-by-side on a cheap Ikea desk in the office he had built in the fireboat's wheel room, glowing behind drawn curtains. Below the desk, an array of blinking lights assured him that his communications were effectively untraceable.

He pushed back his chair, picked up the phone, and called the lead diver. 'Tell me about the samples.'

'We scraped the entire chamber and there are signs of a mould in the corners, though none could be viable after being immersed for so long in salt water.'

'Look again.'

40

MATTHYS'S BOSS was not happy and he could understand why; the monthly statistics should have been on her desk the previous evening and they hadn't been. She would have been even less happy if she knew that he hadn't even started them, which is why he never pointed that out. The problem was, he loved her accent, and so every time she asked him to do something he said yes, even when he knew he'd actually be spending his time looking for St George. Because now he was certain that there was a St George.

He had never managed to track down the mysterious Italian art collector, though the fact that he couldn't find her told him that something was afoot; and in the end it was a just good luck that had turned around his investigation. As usual, he had sat at the back of the weekly briefing on thefts of prominent artworks and antiquities. That morning, the talk had been about a plundered shipwreck recently discovered off the coast of Finland – some fishermen had reported unusual boat activity in the area. It had been a low priority alert, so by the time an EU inspection team arrived, large access holes had already been cut through its exposed flanks and its considerable treasure room had been emptied. Now, everyone was scrambling to cover up their mistakes and determine what, if any, historical value – and no doubt political capital – could still be salvaged.

The project had been codenamed 'Dragon Boat', from the wreck's magnificent figurehead, which had survived in pristine condition. His heart rate hadn't returned to normal since hearing those words. He'd give them the Italian woman's name in a day or two. In the meantime he would try and use their resources to his own end. If he found the gang behind this theft, he would be a very big step closer to catching St George; and then perhaps all would be forgiven.

41

SAM'S PLANE touched down in Gdansk that same morning. He'd had to dump the gun in Riga, but at least that meant that the immigration formalities were minimal.

Spring had broken winter's last resistance and the city was resplendent in sunshine; pastel colours glowed on the gabled merchant houses that lined its streets and their golden embellishments dazzled. Sam was dressed in khaki shorts, a black golf shirt, and flip-flops and he faded into the river of tourists washing through the famous Golden Gate, around the trident-wielding statue of Neptune, and on towards the harbour. Sam's hotel was set three blocks back from that main artery: though still central enough to serve as a base for exploring the Old Town, it offered more privacy.

His room looked like every room in every business hotel around the world; still, he spent ten minutes evaluating its tactical strengths and weaknesses. Feeling secure, he tuned the TV to BBC World News for some background noise, and got to work. He'd picked up a map from reception which he now spread across the desk.

Three minutes later, a big red circle marked his target. He had a problem, though. The name 'Old Town' was something of a misnomer in the case of Gdansk: the city (then the German city of Danzig) had been flattened by Second World War bombing. Almost all of the buildings were, in fact, painstaking replicas. Sam had been worried that any clues would have been lost during the restoration process, but it was worse than that: the spot marked on the map wasn't just a recently restored building, it was a recently restored building of no noticeable historical value – a twenty-storey block of one- and two-bedroom flats.

According to the construction company's website, the development was built on the site of a brewery that had operated there from 1833 to 1939. Playing off of its heritage, the current owners ran a microbrewery in the building's basement, claiming to use the same cellar and the same kettles to make their craft IPAs. If a clue was going to be found at all, that was where it would be. And they ran promotional tours every day so even if it was a bust, a cold glass of Zameczek Lager sounded like a decent consolation.

He had a few hours before the next tour started, so Sam headed to the waterfront for lunch. Over a preparatory beer and a roast-beef sandwich, he decoded the story he hoped he'd get a chance to use. It was another strange one.

It started as a crack in the main road, which became two cracks and then quickly a hole through which a molehill grew; that small annoyance had become a hindrance by the time the mayor went to inspect it at noon; and was growing into a major problem even as he stood and watched. By the time he left to convene a meeting of town elders, an armoured tower barricaded the road, fifty feet high, thirty feet round, and surrounded by a moat.

It was the moat that upset the townsfolk the most; they believed that it went all the way to hell. The mayor couldn't begrudge them their superstitions. Objects thrown into the water never made a splash; they were simply enveloped and then sank, a little too slowly, from view. He was more worried about mundane matters, like the toll that the tower was demanding. The only way to gain safe passage was to throw a silver coin into the moat; those who had tried to pay less had seen their wagons tipped over. Even the fleetest of horses couldn't get past.

The elders agreed to storm the castle that night.

Fifty of Gdansk's fiercest knights gathered at sunset, ready, except for their horses, which refused to approach the spectral citadel. So they were forced to attack on foot, and they made no headway. The invisible forces never let them get close. Tired, dejected, and wounded, they accepted defeat at the stroke of midnight.

The next morning, the mayor received a visit from the captain of the Drachen — docked in the harbour for repairs to their sails — who provided an alternative. In exchange for labour, he said he would return the next day with his bravest men to fight the mysterious foe.

True to his word, the captain and three of his men presented themselves at the moat. The captain embraced each man and, on his signal, they drew their swords and jumped in. The crowd watched them sink, and then disappear. Some of the women started to cry, and with each passing minute, more joined the sorrowful chorus; after five minutes, the crowd was in a frenzy.

Then they gasped as one.

The captain was in front of the tower door, inside the barrier. His lieutenants were standing tall and dry beside him.

The four men stormed in and the air was filled with terrifying screeches. The tower trembled from the battle within, shook, and *then collapsed into rubble. The crowd went silent. Then, as the dust settled, they cheered. The captain and his men were still standing.*

A long table was set up in the street for a party that lasted all of the next day and night. The townsfolk were so grateful that they commissioned a statue in the captain's honour, reputably made by melting all the tribute coins they had recovered when the tower fell.

Sam scanned the story again and then looked at his list of symbols: castle, horse, sword, coin. Check.

The apartment block was a pleasant walk from his hotel, strategically located on the border between the old and new towns; its cellar was cool after the day's sunshine. The walls of six dome-roofed chambers had been knocked through to create a single large space that looked like the inside of an egg carton. The cream plastered walls were hung with black and white photographs and informational plaques. Four dented copper kettles sat in one corner, housing the beer.

Sam had arrived early so he read up on the brewery's history and the reconstruction process. It had been a successful business during the nineteenth century, but it was already in financial difficulty when the buildings were flattened in the war so no one had thought it prudent to revive it. The site then went through a number of tenants, each of whom discarded a little more of its history, until it was just a warehouse. The current owners found the brewing equipment quite by accident while they were replacing sewers. During more careful excavations, they uncovered a flagstone carved with the design after which they named their beer: Zameczek, Polish for 'little castle'.

Sam stared at that picture. Now he was sure of his choice: though the beer's logo was a bright cubist interpretation, the one carved into that flagstone in the photo was an exact copy of the castle symbol in his book.

The plaque was vague on where exactly the flagstone had been found, saying only that it had been discovered among the rubble of a collapsed underground wall. Sam wondered if the hiding place had been opened or destroyed in that collapse, or if by moving the flagstone, they had inadvertently broken the trail. He looked up when a bald man in blue overalls walked in, ready to start the tour.

Sam listened only intermittently, spending most of his time evaluating security features. His ears perked up, though, when the guide mentioned a smuggler's tunnel that ran under the building to the harbour. If it had been dug in the nineteenth century as the guide suggested, it would be of no use to Sam. But if it was older then he just might well be in luck.

Sam savoured the complimentary post-tour beer.

Then as he left, he turned in the doorway to thank the guide. In that instant, shielding it with his body, he stuck a small device on the bottom of the burglar alarm's control panel, which blinked on the wall nearby. That device would record the alarm's activation code when it was keyed in that evening and transmit it to Sam's phone.

42

S AM WALKED into the lobby at ten minutes after midnight, took the lift to the sixth floor, let the doors open and close, and then took it all the way down to the basement-level storerooms. From there, he worked his way to the cellar. He deactivated the alarm in seconds, moved through the tourist area, and headed straight to the old smugglers' tunnel.

Square-cut black bricks lined the ceiling and walls, while the floor was paved with black flagstones, most of which were cracked and scuffed. Sam could smell a history of sea salt in the air. A modern gate closed the tunnel 200 metres in, where the tour had turned around, but Sam soon had it open.

He marched for twenty more minutes before anything changed. The floor's texture changed first, narrow grey bricks sprouted between the flagstones, first filling in the bigger gaps but soon becoming the exclusive form of paving. Then the roof started to dip, to the point that Sam was bent almost double as he walked.

Sam followed the tunnel until it ended at a damp cement wall, a plug inserted to seal the entrance to the harbour. Sam started working back from there. If he was going to find anything tonight, he knew it would be in the oldest section of the tunnel.

It took him an hour to search it thoroughly.

And what he found was subtle. The grey bricks were uneven in size, and haphazardly laid out to compensate for this fact – except at a single point near the middle of the tunnel where the outer edges of the bricks aligned to form a circle about one metre in diameter. Sam swung the duffle bag off his shoulders.

The centuries-old mortar flaked under his chisel. The bricks cracked, too, whenever a blow was misdirected. Sam was expecting the chisel to plunge forward into an open space, but instead, it met sudden resistance.

The clang of metal on metal reverberated through his arm and echoed in the enclosed space. Sam tried again, more tentatively this time. He kept chipping and scraping away and by the time he was done, streaked in grey dust and sweat, he had revealed another bronze disk.

It was as intricately carved as the one in Riga. He could see four concentric circles, each marked along its inner and outer edges with combinations of the symbols with which he was now so familiar. The outermost circle was fixed in place and adorned with a single castle embossed at the two o'clock position. That had to be his starting point.

He rotated the mobile circles, aligning the symbols in the correct order until they told his story. Then he pressed the centre. A familiar ticking and creaking sound preceded four simultaneous thuds and the bronze disk swung open.

43

KALEV WALKED the last kilometre to the apartment, listening to the even clip of his leather-soled shoes on the pavement, letting the journey take half an hour to make sure he wasn't being followed.

'Where is she?' he asked, before the front door had even slammed closed.

His men led him to a small bedroom at the back of the apartment.

She was a beautiful woman; he had noticed her figure while he chased her, of course, but she had a pretty face, too. God, he wished he could smash it. She'd caused him so much trouble. Maybe after Hiko was done with her. Brett was lying on the bed, her eyes closed, but she was awake. Her hands were cuffed behind her back and her left foot was locked to the bed frame by a chain. She was bruised and scratched, but Kalev didn't see any serious injuries.

He uncuffed her hands, tossed a mobile phone and a bottle of water onto the bed and left.

Brett ignored the phone's buzzing until it became less painful to answer than not to. 'What?'

'Bretta, thank you. Let me start by saying that you and I are on the same side, though people will likely have told you otherwise. That's why I called, you see, I would like for us to work together. Actively. I believe we can. And I believe it is in our best interest to do so.'

'It's Brett. And who is this?'

'Ah, I'm sorry, so rude of me, my name is Hiko, though I don't expect that means anything to you. Nevertheless, I am telling the truth when I say that we are well placed to be partners in this quest.'

'Five minutes ago you were trying to kill me. I'm still lying here bound by, I assume, your men, and you want me to believe that you're all of a sudden on my side? Not a chance.'

'Brett, please. I have been forced to do some regrettable things, for which I apologise unreservedly. Please do believe me when I say that I did not act out of malice. But your question is misphrased: it is not sudden that we are on the same side; we have *always* been on the same side. The fiercest rivalry is always between those whose beliefs are ninety-five percent aligned. We are scared of people who are different from us, but we fight against the people who are almost the same. Catholic against Protestant, Sunni against Shi'a; fighting within religions is always more intense that fighting between them. That's you and me.'

'What are you talking about?'

'Brett, I want you to find the treasure. Finding the treasure is more important to me than who finds it. Thus I am more than happy to take on a partner. You bring certain attributes to the table, as do I, so I think a fifty-fifty split is both the simplest and fairest way of doing it. Can you accept my apology and consider these terms?'

'No.'

'Ah.' Hiko's tone didn't change, but she felt the hanging pause was significant. 'I spoke to your friend, by the way. He sold you out.'

'What friend?'

'Lieutenant-Colonel Sam Hansen of Her Majesty's Special Reconnaissance Regiment.'

Brett laughed. 'Sam? He's no friend of mine. And whatever he told you, you can assume is a lie.'

'He said you have the dragons.'

'A case in point. I don't have them, he does.' *And the book,* though there was no need to volunteer that information.

'I know. We searched your hotel room. The point is, without me you're alone in this mess.'

Brett fought to control her breathing. If they had searched her hotel room, had they found Patrick? Where was he and what condition was he in?

Hiko seemed to take her silence as a signal to continue. 'You and I have both been robbed by the same man. And, I'm embarrassed to say, he now has the best hand at the table. Do you play poker, Brett? If we continue to wrestle over the scraps, he'll walk away with the pot. If we team up, we can win. I can make available a lot of resources that you would find very useful.'

'No.'

'I understand. Rather the devil you know, right? But tell me this, what happened when you first approached that underground chamber in Tallinn?'

'He tried to shoot me,' Brett conceded. 'So did your guys.'

'Who fired the first shots? And who was acting in self-defence?'

Brett thought back, it could have been Sam.

Hiko seemed comfortable in the long silences. 'And what happened after that, Brett?'

'What are you proposing?'

'My men are not far behind him. I have watchers in every Hanseatic town from Novgorod to Bruges, from Bergen to Krakow. So he was spotted. An hour ago in Gdansk. My men there will follow him to the next site and call us in. I'll let you pick up the search from there.'

'And then?'

'And then we split the treasure.'

'That easy?'

'There is one artefact I desire. I ask to be given the opportunity to make the first pick. Thereafter, we can divide the rest. Are you happy with that? And you can take public credit for finding the wreck, if you wish; I don't have the sort of name that belongs in the press.'

'I did find the wreck.'

'That's what I said.'

'Never mind. More importantly, how do I know you won't turn around and kill me when we find the treasure so you can take it all?'

'Can I assume that we have a deal?'

44

COLD AIR seeped out of the tunnel and settled around his
ankles. Sam peeked inside. The walls were hard-packed
dirt, the roof so low that he would have to remove his duffle
bag and push it ahead of him. He had no choice, so he climbed
in, trusting it would take him somewhere worthwhile.

It was monotonous at first: shove the duffle bag a metre,
crawl, shove, crawl – until the bag suddenly wasn't there. He
heard a splash a second later and edged forward, gingerly,
leading with his fingertips.

Sam lowered his head all the way through the hole in the
tunnel's floor that had swallowed the bag; and, head upside
down, watched ripples expand out across the surface of a dark
pool. The room he was looking into was the size of a double-car
garage and, as far as he could tell, he was at its centre. Struc-
turally, it echoed the brewery's domed cellars. He reversed into
the tunnel and contorted his body around. If he was going to
get wet, he'd at least need to protect his headlamp.

Once he was in position, Sam lowered his legs over the edge,
slowly, waiting to reach the limit of his stretch before letting
go, kicking already to minimise how far he sank.

The water was freezing, and for a minute, he could do nothing but gasp and look around.

Sam swum across to his floating bag and pulled out the other torch he'd brought along. It sparked for a moment before spluttering out. He gave it a shake and this time, the beam glowed more permanently. Dark shapes undulated below the surface, though nothing broke through the surface.

Sam swam a grid over the flooded emptiness. It was painfully slow work. He had to paddle, wait for the water to settle, search its depths, then repeat the process five metres further along.

It took him fifteen freezing minutes to make his first find: a structure three metres below, with crenellated parapets lining its ten-metre circumference. He circled it, but that was all he could see from there. He would have to get closer. He tied the torch to the duffle's strap, aiming it down as best he could, and dived.

Some light accompanied him, revealing unbroken brick walls before hitting its limits and leaving him alone in the dark. Sam kept going, his hands discovering more of the same hard stone walls as he kicked down. He hadn't reached the bottom before the need for air turned him around and he shot to the surface.

Sam took four deep breaths and regained his composure.

This time when he dived, his eyes were closed from the start. His fingers played over the stones like a piano virtuoso.

When he popped back up, he was smiling. He relished a challenge. Sam moved a few degrees around its circumference and dived again, tickling more metres of solid wall. He surfaced, moved further around, and dived again.

Sam's fingers traced a textured path, until he felt nothing at all; an entrance. Two firm kicks later, he reached the floor. He opened his eyes but to no avail. Sam had to rely on his cold-numbed sense of touch to measure the door frame. His lungs protested, but he held on and probed hollow space beyond the door with his feet. It could accommodate him, that was for sure. He *had* to surface now, yet he stayed where he was, forcing his heart rate down.

Sam counted out the seconds while his lungs screamed.

When he finally gave in, he had a plan. He'd been able to stay under for two minutes. It was almost enough time to explore the tower . . . if he had a light.

He was an idiot. He'd not thought to bring a waterproof torch, and he had to have light or he might never find his way out; so his plan revolved around bodging the headlamp into a dive lamp.

Sam unzipped one of the backpack's side pockets and removed two plastic Ziploc bags. He turned on his headlamp and dropped it into a bag, sealed it, and then dropped that package into the second bag, which he filled with a breath of air before closing; to keep it buoyant. It might work; he only needed the seal to hold for a few minutes, after all.

Sam dived again and this time when he reached the door, he went in headfirst, taking a quick look around the interior. He was right, it extended all the way up. Sam released the glowing package and watched as it rose in a spiral of bubbles. As the headlamp floated higher, a warm gold light filled the tower, bouncing and settling against the ceiling thirty seconds later.

Sam kicked back to the surface to prepare for what he hoped would be his final dive.

45

S AM SUCKED in a dozen fast breaths and with a powerful kick, dove downwards again. Everything was on the line, now. When his hands found the doorway, he tumble-turned into the tower and allowed his natural buoyancy to carry him towards its glowing upper section; small bubbles trickled out of his nose, racing him to his goal.

The interior walls told the story of the mysterious tower as it climbed upwards, climaxing around him as he rose. Life beat in the details, growing more urgent with every centimetre. He imagined he could hear the clash of sword on shield. He even reached out to stroke the muzzle of a carved horse as he passed it, just to see if it felt like stone or hair. A bronze fire grew from thin bronze flames in the windows into a conflagration of swords and spirits that swarmed the top two metres. Sam neglected his lungs' cries for air as he rotated slowly. It was becoming more difficult to tame his pulse. There was no amber globe. His vision started to narrow. But there was not even a gap where a globe might once have been. Pins and needles sparked in his fingertips as he turned a second circuit.

There was still no dragon. Sam's lungs and heart fought each other to tear through his chest, his field of vision had been crushed to a tube of monochromatic blurs, and survival instinct pleaded his eyes downwards, towards the exit and a chance of safety. But there had to be a dragon.

Sam reached above his head for the floating light, but the bag stayed where it was. Stuck. He tugged it. It didn't move. He had to be careful; two thin layers of plastic were all that was keeping it isolated from the water. He looked up, straight into the light, and saw the dragon, embedded in a nook at the crest of the ceiling, hidden until then by the floating headlamp itself.

Sam ripped it out, no longer concerned when the bag tore and darkness flooded in. He had the dragon. Pushing off the ceiling, he kicked for the door.

Sam was in a slow-motion race against his own body, which felt like it was shutting down at high speed. He grabbed the stone wall with his free hand and pulled as he kicked. His eyes were closed and his nerves dulled by the cold, only his ears betrayed this cocoon of sensory deprivation, shrilling with a high-pitched buzz.

Then his hand found the exit and hope bloomed.

Sam wrapped an arm around the door's lintel and hauled his body out. With two tired kicks he shot upwards. The hunt wasn't over.

46

BRETT HAD been held in the room for over a day. She hadn't been maltreated, but she had been bored. A noise shook her awake. A second crash. Then the door broke open, revealing one of her jailers briefly haloed in a spray of broken furniture, before his body thudded down next to hers. She pulled at her bindings, twisting to catch more of the frenzied movement in the main room. Fists, elbows, and projectiles collided in the limited space. Then the chaos rolled out of sight again.

A shout and a dull thud preceded the arrival of a second body; though this time her neighbour was temporary and he was soon back on his feet. Brett yelled in surprise. It was Patrick. His hair was unruly and matted with sweat and blood. His skin was flushed. And he was stark naked.

He didn't seem to notice her as he bounced on the spot, weight forward, his hands raised, and his eyes locked on the large man striding into the bedroom, armed with a knife. The man stopped two metres away and waited there, staring at Patrick.

Patrick held his fighter's pose.

The other man took a quick step and lunged at Patrick with the knife. Patrick dodged left and struck with a lightning jab that shook a thin trickle of blood from the man's nose. Patrick skipped past him as he reeled, back into the corridor. The man he had left behind leered at Brett as he licked the blood off his top lip, and then hurried out of the room to add to the destructive soundtrack: clattering glasses, a bottle breaking, and the clash of steel.

Brett heard a scream.

Another metallic crash.

Bilingual curses.

Another blood-curdling scream.

When Brett saw Patrick again, a curtain of blood covered his ribs and his kitchen knife-wielding assailant was on the attack. Patrick ducked under the blade's flashing arc and rolled back as a heavy boot swung towards his head. Patrick sprung up from his crouch, aiming the top of his head straight at his attacker's throat.

The man turned his shoulder just in time to absorb the impact, and together the two men crashed to the ground. The knives skittered loose. The men's eyes met. Patrick scampered left, going for the knife, the other man right, collecting a fresh blade from the countertop.

Patrick faked a lunge. The other man didn't buy it. He smiled, then thrust his knife towards Patrick's chest in a brutally swift move. Patrick turned just in time, like a matador sidestepping a charge. Patrick swung his elbow back, but the other man had already stepped out of range.

Brett watched from the doorway, the chain digging into her ankle as she pulled for a better angle. Patrick swung again, this time with the knife. The man dodged the blade and counter-attacked with better results, slicing Patrick's bicep.

Patrick changed tactics with a high spinning kick. It glanced off the man's shoulder and clipped his head, but failed to put him down.

Both men kept moving. Brett lost sight of the action again. She heard a fall and furniture break, followed by the thud of flesh and the clang of clashing blades.

Patrick was chasing the other man when they came back into view. Both men were breathing heavily. Both were bleeding. And that's when Brett attacked.

In two strides she was out of the room. She leapt onto the man's back, wrapped her arms around his head, and gouged at his eyes. He was far stronger and easily shook her loose; then he unleashed a backhanded strike that sent her crashing into the couch. He turned back to face Patrick. By then it was too late, Patrick plunged his knife into the man's calf, and followed that up with an elbow to the back of his head, stopping the embryonic scream in his opponent's mouth and ending the fight.

He and Brett were free.

Brett was too sore to get off the floor; all she could manage was to roll her head towards Patrick. 'So, is this how you apologise for treating me like a baby?'

'Would you accept it if it was?'

'No.'

'I'm sorry, Brett. This is your, thing, not mine, and I had no right to try to protect you from it.'

'Apology accepted, but. . . .'

'But what?'

'But what? But what are you doing naked?'

Patrick chuckled. 'Oh, sorry you had to see that.'

'If you really were sorry, you'd at least be pulling your pants back on.'

Patrick gave Brett a big grin, while making no move to dress. 'So how did you get free?'

Brett held up a keyring. 'These were in the pocket of that guard you left in my room, back there. Couldn't have happened to a nicer man in my opinion, but let's not ignore your nakedness. . . .'

'You're right. It would be an awful shame to ignore it.'

'That's not how I meant it, and you know it. Put on your clothes and explain to me why I even need to say those words.'

'Right, I was getting to that. When I was working in Albania I became friendly with one of my bodyguards and he once mentioned that the scariest fight he'd ever been in was with a crazy naked guy. He said that being naked signals to your opponent that you have nothing to lose, as it were.'

'Dress and speak, Patrick, dress and speak.'

'No, wait, it makes sense. Also, it puts your opponent off something rotten, especially the sort of macho alpha male that gravitates towards a career as a soldier of fortune, there's a sort of latent homophobia there that prevents them from focusing on anything below your waist and that allows you—'

Brett averted her eyes. She also considered her options. She'd just been presented with a perfectly respectable exit point and a clear example of the risks she was facing. She should just call that Hiko fellow, or wait until he called her, give him the book and be done with it. This hunt was not worth her life, or the life of her best friend. 'Do you think we should stop?'

'What, now? Just when things are starting to get exciting?'

'I'm serious, Patrick. They're not getting exciting, I almost got you killed. And for what? To prove a point? To find the gold? I don't need the gold, you don't need the gold. This is just me running around on some selfish ego trip, isn't it? Millions of people have dealt with worse setbacks without resorting to some melodramatic quest.'

'You need to be brave, Brett, and follow this through.'

'You're not understanding me, Patrick. I'm not scared for myself. Look at you: you're going to need twenty, maybe thirty stitches to fix that cut and you got lucky. An inch higher and you'd be dead. That's why I want to stop.'

'That's exactly what I mean: being brave isn't about being willing to put your own life at risk, that's actually pretty easy, you never have to face the consequences of a mistake when you're dead; no, being brave is about being willing to stand side by side with people you care about when they're likely to pay the price for any mistake you make. Trusting yourself to make the right decision in those situations, that's being brave.'

'Patrick. . . .'

'And it's been bloody fun, hasn't it?'

Brett laughed. 'It has been fun, I suppose. Okay, let's go check out that gate of yours.'

47

MATTHYS HAD taken the lead investigator to lunch and had ended up paying, which wasn't how it was supposed to work since Matthys was the one who had brought the scoop on the Italian woman's involvement. But the task team had its eyes on someone a little more sinister: a Finnish hitman. Still, while Matthys' information hadn't gotten him a free lunch, it had at least gotten him access to the investigation's findings.

It was amazing the information a little physical evidence could provide. They had commandeered forensic teams from Finland, Sweden, and Holland. Collaborating, those teams had already matched the wreck's coordinates to a series of phone calls. Though the calls were encrypted, they had been able to infer the gang's location and movements.

So far, it looked like two teams. The first team had assembled in Finland, spent four days near the wreck, and then moved to Estonia and dispersed. The second team had replaced them at the wreck, spent two days there, and then dissipated throughout Europe. Both teams had discarded their phones exactly ten days after they first appeared on the grid, suggesting a pre-agreed strategy.

The bosses were now focusing on Estonia, where those final calls had been made. But Matthys knew St George wasn't in Europe. No one had seen him and nothing had been stolen. So while the others ran in circles, he would dive into the lesser-called locations. Why, he wondered for example, had someone in each team received a call from the same phone in Hong Kong. . . .

48

KALEV WAS in an awkward position. He had caught the girl, but he hadn't exactly made himself indispensable. Hiko was talking to Brett now and if he got what he was after. . . .

Which is why he was standing at the base of the scaffolding that had been conveniently erected around the Holsten Gate. He could think of only one reason for Brett to be in Lübeck: to look for those amber dragons. And this was the most likely location in town. He had a short time while Brett was waylaid and if he was going to jump ahead in this race, it must be now. The scaffolding rattled as he climbed, ringing like a bell in the quiet morning.

Kalev focussed on the two bands of terracotta tiles that circled the gate, alternating in groups of eight around the gate's girth, separated each time by two guards bearing a single shield emblazoned with Lübeck's coat of arms.

Kalev started with the lower band, staring at each tile in the stark light of his headlamp, willing a pattern to appear.

After an hour, he was almost back at his starting point. The groups of eight had to be significant, and the lilies and thistles they were decorated with could be, too. But what did they signify?

He wasn't despondent yet, though. He hadn't expected it to be easy. He had drawn a grid of small squares and as he passed each tile, he marked the corresponding square with a shorthand code: a cross for the lilies, a horizontal line for the thistles, and a vertical for the lattice. He'd let the computer look for more subtle patterns later.

By the time Kalev neared the end of the second band, he had to wipe sweat from his eyes before each new tile. The day had become hot and, together with the repetitive view, it was fertilising a migraine.

The drum of an approaching truck forced him to ignore his discomfort and hurry through the last fifteen tiles. As it bounced onto the pavement, clattering tools in the load bed, Kalev jumped to the ground and jogged away. He checked his watch: a quarter to nine. In Germany, even municipal employees were punctual. Kalev took cover in a nearby hedge and watched them prepare.

Patrick and Brett arrived at the gate ten minutes before nine, and were also impressed to see the two workers already there.

'*Guten morgen.*'

Patrick didn't speak any German, but a nod and a proffered cigarette appeared to be sufficient atonement; they lit up and switched to accented English. Patrick had chosen to visit during the day because, while the night offered a blanket of anonymity, it would also have made their presence less explainable to any nosey passersby. Hiding in plain sight was always better, and these two men were his bright orange camouflage. Patrick pulled on matching overalls and a white hardhat, while Brett pretended to fill out paperwork on a clipboard.

According to their cover story, they were from the European Union's Committee for the Preservation of Significant Monuments, there to ensure no damage occurred during a cleaning operation, and the European Union never sent one bureaucrat when they could send two.

Patrick would be the first one up, he'd scan the gate for 'existing damage' and the two men would start cleaning behind him.

The exterior of the gate was a huge surface to cover and it took Patrick an hour just to reach the first band of tiles. He'd always assumed that he would have the best chance of finding a clue there, but he knew he'd be plagued by doubt if he skipped a section, and it would have been harder to explain to the workers.

Patrick moved along the line, staring, counting, and filming as he went. It took another hour to complete the full circuit, by which time he had learnt nothing. The eagle that decorated the heraldic shield on one tile might almost look a little bit like a dragon, if he was grasping at straws, and there was a single row of seven lilies, although that was more likely to be an oversight on the restorers' part than a clue. In any case, none of the tiles, nor their preceding or succeeding neighbours, had done anything when he pressed it.

It was four o'clock by the time Patrick gave up. He had nothing to show for his sunburn and backache except a clean national icon. He wondered if the city would appreciate that. Patrick thanked the two men for their day's work, gave them the last of the cigarettes, and went to find Brett. She was now supervising from an outdoor table at a café across the road.

She would argue that it had a great view of the gate.

49

'THOSE TILES, with the guards and the shield, are Lübeck's coat of arms. They're all over town.' Patrick said. They were in his hotel room reviewing the footage he'd captured earlier.

'Yeah, I saw them above the old bridge near the gate. What about the other tiles?'

'I still don't know. Might have been a favourite of some dead king for all I know. In any case, if they're also scattered around town, then I guess we're most likely to spot the thistle. I assume you don't see too many of those in German symbolism.'

'Is that what you think we need to do? Look for these symbols on major buildings?' Brett was sitting cross-legged on the floor, thumbing through a pile of books as he watched the screen.

'It's all I can think of. It might give us another reference point, at least.'

'Is there anything interesting in the rest of this video?'

'I don't know.' Patrick's eyes were locked on the screen. 'Maybe I missed something the first time around.'

'And what about the missing lily, shouldn't we be looking for that, not a thistle?

'Well, yes, I suppose. But there could be a million reasons why that one was missing and even more reasons for a lily to be on a building; I just thought a thistle would stand out more. So look for any of the symbols and we'll go from there.'

While Patrick watched the rest of the video, Brett scanned through a coffee table book of Lübeck, which they had bought that afternoon. The Holsten Gate was beautifully featured, as were most of the town's important buildings. All were photographed and explained, albeit with more emphasis on artistic angles and warm light than on historical facts. Brett saw a few pictures of the coat of arms and none of the other symbols. When she looked up, Patrick was still engrossed in the jerky progression of tiles, so she moved to the next book in the stack. That one focused on churches in the region and it, too, left her no more enlightened.

'You can turn that off, I've solved the riddle, I am a genius.' Brett said.

Patrick looked across to her. The pile of read books had grown taller than the pile of unread books before a snippet of information had caught Brett's eye. She was looking at a sketch of a short, wide bridge, edged on either side by stepped balustrades that bowed outwards at the bridge's midpoint to form two Juliet balconies. Brett held up the book and prodded the picture. The interior of one of those balconies was decorated with a chiselled bouquet of thistles.

'You're a genius? Wasn't I the one who said it would be a thistle? What does it say?'

'Ha, you had a one-in-four chance of guessing right. Anyway, listen to this, there used to be four bridges into Lübeck's Old Town. The one near the Holsten Gate is the only one still standing, but this is a sketch of the southern bridge, based on evidence from pieces fished out of the river and a few paintings that predate its collapse.'

'So, you're thinking—'

'Yeah, if two of the bridges were decorated with motifs from the gate, then the missing two were likely the same.'

'You might be right.'

'I think "genius" was the word I used. . . .'

Sam forced himself alert. His plane had been delayed and the airport was quiet when he landed in Lübeck. He collected his suitcase from the conveyor belt and stayed near the back of the bubble of disembarking passengers, giving everyone in the terminal a quick once over.

Seeing no threat, he joined the taxi queue.

50

A STOOPED man pushed a room service trolley down an empty corridor, checking the numbered doors as he shuffled past. Halfway down, he took a key card from his pocket, glanced left and right, unlocked the door and slipped inside, pulling it closed behind him.

Kalev's threw off his disguise with relief. He poured himself a large cup of coffee, and slid into a chair in front of the four monitors: they showed an empty corridor, a bustling lobby, and two empty stairwells. Then he turned to the man next to him, 'Is he still in there?'

The chubby man in a tucked-in short-sleeve, button-down shirt blinked at Kalev through trendy eyeglasses. 'Yes.'

'You can go now.'

The man nodded, stood, shrugged on a black biker jacket, and left.

Kalev was in the room across from Sam's. Motion-activated sensors covered the corridor and exit points and would alert him if Sam left, but Kalev didn't want to leave his fate entirely in the hands of their infrared beams, so he watched the monitors himself.

He had watched them for two hours without seeing any movement from Sam. He was probably asleep. A chime from Kalev's watch meant that it was time to check in with Hiko. He had hoped to have something concrete to report on, but he couldn't afford to be late, so he poured himself a fifth coffee and dialled. The call was answered before the second ring. 'The operation is underway, sir.'

'I need a delivery date, Kalev.'

'I am watching his room now. I have men posted at the front and rear exits. Two more in the street. He can't go anywhere without us knowing about it.'

'Kalev, it seems like you're always waiting for someone else to make the next move. Call me tomorrow morning with a result.'

'Sir.' Kalev killed the call and swore.

Sam always woke at 4 AM. He watched the empty street outside for five minutes before taking a cold shower; by quarter past the hour, he was sitting on the bed wearing the hotel robe and slippers with the book and a map of Lübeck in front of him. He sorted through the keys and picked one, fitted it over the cross that marked the starting point, and circled his target.

Still, the location was patently wrong, unless the spot the key identified hadn't always been under water.

Ten minutes later, Sam was dressed and ready to go, the book locked in the room safe. He stashed the duffle bag in the wardrobe and locked it, threw a small backpack over his shoulder and eased the door open. He checked the corridor, jogged to the stairwell and stopped, listening for followers, then bounded down the steps in short, fast strides.

Kalev's eyes clicked open when the alarm sounded. It was time. He sent a message telling his technician to break down the listening post, did his best to smooth his rumpled suit with his hands, buffed a shine in his wingtips with a quick rub against his yellow, red, and blue striped socks, and opened the door.

A bridge had once crossed the river, right where the key said the dragon would be. It had taken Sam an hour to find a historical reference to it – it had been destroyed 200 years ago and had never been rebuilt. He hoped its fate hadn't harmed the dragon, but since every other clue had been secreted away in an underground chamber, it was possible that this dragon waited for him, submerged but intact.

The morning's combination of cool air and bright sunshine was invigorating. Sam waved to a lone hotel gardener as he jogged into the street. He took a moment to get his bearings, then headed due east. The quaintness of the Old Town transitioned into suburbia as roads straightened out and franchised businesses took over. The working half of the city was rising: cars pulled out of overnight parking spaces and coffee and pastry-laden office drones emerged from every bakery and cafe he passed.

Kalev kept his team at a distance, making sure they switched positions often to avoid detection. So far, his quarry had kept to main roads, making it easy for them.

Patrick knocked and waited. He thought of knocking again, but decided to give her some time.

Brett opened the door a minute later, probably only because she smelt the coffee he was holding, 'Black with one sugar?'

'As you like it.'

Brett took the cup from Patrick. He was dressed in navy blue cargo pants and a wine red V-neck jumper inspired by Sean Connery in *Goldfinger*, but she looked even more like a film star in head-to-toe dark-grey yoga gear. Though she had found the time to accessorise it with gold braid epaulets. Brett's hair was still damp from her shower, but her appearance gave no other indications of having just woken up. She took a slow sip of the strong brew. 'You don't know what you're missing.'

Patrick shuddered. 'The only thing you'll ever see me drinking black is Guinness, and even for me it's a little early for that. Unless you insist. Are you insisting? Because for you. . . .'

Brett gave his arm a friendly punch. 'Come, let's go.' She grabbed her bag and followed him to the hotel lobby.

It had taken them until well past midnight to identify the locations of the two fallen bridges and even then, they hadn't been able to ascertain which had been decorated with the lilies. Which was why, after just a few hours sleep and despite Brett's usual disdain for early mornings, they were already on the move.

51

BRETT AND Patrick headed east. If they didn't find anything there, they would still be able to search the western site before lunch. The streets were quiet; only a few joggers and a scattering of workaholics were out this early.

Kalev's men were half a kilometre away. They reported Sam was patrolling an area near the river, looking for something. Kalev needed to be there when Sam found whatever it was.

Kalev pushed his chair back from the table, leaving his untouched coffee – he wasn't going to pay for something he didn't drink.

Sam counted his paces, back and forth. If he was right, the bridge would have crossed the river within a few metres of where he now stood. Though a paved jogging path had smoothed over any remains, one hint remained: two ancient oak trees grew five metres on either side of him and were mirrored by two cousins on the opposite bank. Sam allowed himself to imagine their ancestors shading the bridge's entrance and exit. It wasn't impossible. He stared into the dull river, but even a fairground fortune teller would struggle to divine anything in the opaque water.

Sam kicked the ground and sifted the handful of loosened dirt, keeping the bigger pebbles. He tossed one after the other into the stream. They sank pointlessly. He looked around for something bigger. A quarter brick followed the pebbles and it, too, was lost.

'I should be throwing those stones at him,' Brett whispered to Patrick.

He put out a restraining hand, though he knew she'd never storm over; the best time to strike back was yet to come.

Sam looked up when a shadow cut his path: he was surrounded. Outnumbered five to one, he raised his hands. The men to his left and right stood rigid, answering to the tall blond man striding towards him.

'Put your arms down. Drop the bag and step away,' Kalev ordered.

'And then? What do I get out of this deal?'

'This is an opportunity for you to walk away unharmed.'

'But I am already unharmed and currently en route to the treasure, so I fail to see the merits of your proposal.'

Kalev drew his pistol. 'Give me the dragons and the maps you used to get here.'

Sam's eyes wandered beyond Kalev to the line of gun-toting soldiers, and then his shoulders slumped. He twisted to take off his backpack but as Kalev stepped forward, Sam spun back and spat into his outstretched hand. Kalev swung his pistol in a fast arc but Sam kept spinning so the blow that followed was a glancing one. Sam hit the ground bleeding, but already in a sprinter's starting position. He rocketed towards the river, getting three strides in before the first shot came, four more before the gunmen found their range, by which time he was airborne.

Bullets chased him through the air and then through the water, tracing effervescent trails as he sunk from view.

52

S AM KICKED downwards to stay out of the bullets' range, while unzipping his backpack and removing an underwater torch – this time he had come prepared. Since he had to stay under, he might as well look for the clue. Sam followed the path his torch cut through the murk. He gave himself a minute, if he found nothing by then he would go dark, drift, and surface as far downstream as possible.

The sediment stirred into a lace curtain that distorted, but didn't hide, buried shapes. He kicked again and jabbed his fingers deeper into the mud, feeling a solidness an inch below.

Time and air were running out.

Sam swam along the raised scar of the fallen bridge.

Tiny air bubbles escaped his mouth and trickled upwards, his lungs had become an egg timer. It ran out just as a circular pile of stones rose into view, pushing through the riverbed. Sam shot upwards, gulping three seconds of fresh clean air before duck-diving back under when bullets spat in the water around him.

His fingers found the pile of masonry again, exploring it and measuring the gaps that linked larger pieces.

Double or nothing. Sam squeezed through the first hole big enough to take him.

Brett was heading right into the maelstrom. She didn't even slow down when the gunmen turned to face her. Instead, she ran through their agitated ranks and dived into the river.

Patrick followed, two steps behind.

He heard three more splashes as he chased her wake.

A few tons of stone was jenga-ed above, below, and around Sam. He could see a bigger cavity one level lower, but he couldn't see a safe way to get there, just the narrowest of channels between three overlapping boulders.

He went for it.

With his hands stretched straight out and his head tucked in, he dolphin-kicked downwards. His right hand slipped in, then his left, his elbow caressing stone as he twisted. Nothing moved. Not the rock. Not him. A nervous dolphin kick. Nothing. He was wedged. He kicked again, harder this time. He was still stuck. Panic threatened to control his actions. This time, as Sam kicked he also shrugged his shoulders. Time stopped as he felt something moving, was it him or the pile of stones?

The formation held and Sam's next kick sent him into what must once have been a stairwell. He had a minute of air left, no more, and there was now no way he could go back; so he searched for the only thing that could save him now: another way out. At least he had reached the bottom. Sam wiped away six inches of historic grime, and caught a glint of bronze.

Overriding all instincts, he forced himself to remain stationary as the silt settled around him. The image on the disk was becoming clearer with each second, but he couldn't have more than twenty of those seconds left. He saw a ship. A horse. And a guillotine.

Brett popped up next to Patrick and panted instructions in between breaths. Patrick had never been much of a swimmer, the Irish weather generally not being conducive to the pursuit of water sports, so after he had surfaced the first time without being shot at, he had stayed there, treading water while Brett explored the riverbed on her own.

'Sam's right below us now. I think he found it. Take a deep breath and then follow me down. And keep calm, panic uses more air.'

Patrick said a quick prayer to St Jude and complied as best he could. While Brett bored into the murky water with easy, powerful kicks, he lagged behind with short, choppy ones. Silt roiled in the water, swirling through and around a pile of fallen building blocks, lit from below.

Brett pierced a gap in the stone rattan as soon as she reached it. Patrick paused. He looked down and saw Brett's lithe figure slip untroubled through a maze of stone and space, towards the source of the glow. Patrick found the courage to follow her, just as Brett continued into a yet-deeper space.

As Patrick chased her, his world imploded.

Water rushed past him, dragging him down with it. He fought for control against a current that bashed him into the huge stones and wrenched him through the gaps; and then it pulled the stones down around him, the boulders collapsing like dominoes. And all the while, the water maintained its unrepentant pull, dragging him deeper, even as he watched the chaos through his feet.

53

S AM PRESSED the guillotine; and then the crown as soon as
it cleared into view. The lock clicked. But there was no
movement. The disk was stuck. The water pressure was keeping
it plugged into the riverbed. He hadn't thought of that. Sam
worked his diving knife between the disk and the floor and
tried to lever it out. He used all his upper body strength. He
even kicked himself downwards. The disk didn't move. And
his breath was exhausted. Locked or unlocked, it didn't matter.
There was no way he was going to shift the disk.

Then he was falling through air. His trying to lift the disk
must have stressed the ancient stone lip on which it rested.
While Sam had fought to lift the disk, the river had fought to
push it in. The river had won.

Sam drew in an instinctive, gorgeous breath as he plunged
into the empty core of a spiral stairwell. Stone steps blitzed
through his peripheral vision as he fell. He threw out a hand
and his fingers strummed over the first dozen of these lifelines.
Then he caught one. The cold, dry stone cut into his hand, the
weight of his body wrenched his shoulder and his momentum
swung him into the wall.

Another step provided a foothold and, at last, a chance to rest. Sam looked around. He was in tubular stairwell, surely inside the collapsed bridge's central column. The waterfall thundered behind him.

There was nothing above him, so Sam started to climb down. A lateral tunnel branched off, he had no choice but to take it; the sound of water on stone was already being replaced by the sound of water on water, his cell was flooding.

This was nothing like the quiet, haunting experienced of diving the wreck of the *Drachen*. That had carried a passive sense of foreboding, a reasonable understanding of the risks of solo wreck diving infused with some extra spookiness, thanks to the stares of long-dead skeletons: what she felt now was an active and physical terror. More like that night in the woods. Brett was being slammed against stones. Those stones were being slammed against each other. Everything was moving. Everything was at the mercy of the water.

And then she was falling.

To her left, she saw a brief flash of light, but even as she reached for it, it was gone. Then pain exploded in her hand. And again. Cutting her. Her elbow struck a wall. A sharply-angled stone crashed into her knee, then clipped her wrist and burst through her grasp. The next step caught her ankle. Her body tumbled over and then fell again, headfirst now. Then her shoulder hit a step, flipping her again. Brett bounced and threw out her right hand, and this time when her fingers caught hold of the step she didn't let go.

Brett's body was saturated with pain and it took her a moment to fully appreciate the fact that she was breathing again. At least she was out of the water, though its presence remained oppressive in the small space; it thundered past, splashing somewhere deep below her, its spray wetting her back.

And then Patrick's limp body dropped past.

Sam sprinted along the tunnel. It was comfortably proportioned and precisely level. Unfortunately so. Sam needed it to climb. If it didn't, once the river had filled the stairwell, it would come after him. It was basic hydrodynamics.

Brett first noticed the sound because it was different, a break from the monotonous white noise that rumbled around her. It was faint, but she was certain it was there. Brett listened. It was quiet again. And then she heard it for sure.

'Patrick? Are you okay?'

If he had answered, his response had been lost in the cacophony. She had no light to see him with and no rope to drop, so her only option was to climb down.

Brett could hear grunts and coughing so Patrick had to be close. She knelt down and swung her right hand in a hopeful flight pattern through the empty space below. She felt water, then Patrick grabbed her wrist.

'Three. Two. One.' Brett was jerked forward by Patrick's weight, but his other hand soon found a step and relieved her of the burden. 'Thank you.' His voice was hoarse.

'Can you climb?'

'Christ, can't I take a break for a minute?'

Brett understood his exhaustion, but the water was already wetting their boots. 'You need to come, even moving slowly is better than standing still.'

'Who said that first, Confucius?'

'Shut up and climb.'

Kalev sat on a bench a kilometre downriver, pretending to read a newspaper like a cold war spy. His dive crew had reported back: his targets were likely dead; he didn't care about that, Hiko wouldn't believe him, regardless, but Kalev had to assume that they had been aiming for the next dragon and he did care about that; finding that was his only hope of redemption. So right now his researchers were reviewing every blueprint they could get their hands on, and soon they'd find another way into whatever lay below the river.

54

THEY RAN now, without any knowledge of what lay ahead, measuring their progress by the level of the water soaking their feet: when the water passed their ankles, it was a nuisance; when it reached midcalf, it was a hindrance; when it passed their knees, it became a burden. Brett tried to ignore the trend's obvious conclusion.

'We haven't seen him.'

'What?' The sound of Patrick's voice, so suddenly beside her, made Brett stumble, not because he'd spoken loudly, he hadn't, he still couldn't, but because his voice had snapped her back to reality and that was a heavy weight to bear.

'You said you'd seen Sam head this way. Well, if we haven't found him coming back, we can assume this route isn't a dead end.'

'Or that it's a very long dead end. Or maybe I didn't see him? I don't know anymore. A flash of light during that fall? It could all have been in my head!'

'But the tunnel was there.'

'That could be luck.'

They slowed to a trudge as the water rode up their thighs. It was now deep enough to host temperamental currents, which pushed and pulled on a whim, tripping Brett and Patrick whenever they lost concentration. Brett stayed down after her second fall, floating, letting the water carry her along. It was an uncomfortable and unpredictable means of transport, but it was also a relief to stop fighting for a minute.

When Brett stood back up, she regretted her earlier moodiness. 'We still haven't passed him,' she shouted back to Patrick. He was right, the longer they went without passing Sam, the more likely it was that there was another way out. It was just a question of whether they would beat the water to it.

Brett's improved mood subsided as the water continued to rise. It was getting choppier, too. Small waves reflected off the walls, slapping a sad and repetitive soundtrack. It was now so deep that if her feet reached the paved floor, the water pawed at her chest and it just seemed easier to swim. Patrick followed her lead as best he could.

And the water kept rising.

It rose until Brett's hands brushed the ceiling with each stroke.

Now Brett had to float on her back just to steal a breath. Drifting with the current, suddenly she sensed emptiness above.

Brett ducked under the surface and searched the swirling water for a point of traction. When she felt the squared edge of a stone step, she scrambled upwards on her hands and knees. Patrick was more lethargic, but the rising water forced him to act.

The stairs climbed steeply, and seemingly continuously, testing the resolve of tired legs. But after fifteen minutes they came to a small circular landing of moss-cracked stones. On the far side an arched doorway opened into a plain chapel: three wooden pews facing a marble altar; painted windows decorated the walls and, although time had reimagined their scenes in pastel shades, they must once have been as vibrant as backlit stained glass.

Brett pointed to a damp path trodden across the dusty floor; Sam had passed that way. And he had removed something from the altar: Brett noted two clean indentations in the red and white layer of spilled candle wax that gave the granite surface its Gaudi-esque shape.

The footprints led them into a room of nauseating form and proportion: long and pyramidal, its deep black surfaces had been polished to a high sheen that reflected a single splash of light in infinite ways. Thirty metres away a man stood, staring at a sloping wall, mumbling to himself.

Patrick touched Brett's arm and signalled her back towards the wall. She followed only when it was clear that he was retreating, too.

They took cover in the dark corner where the floor met the diagonal wall, and crawled towards the man. Brett couldn't make out specific words, but in the wash of his torch, she could guessed what he was doing: counting the symbols – they ran along every surface, the same symbols that decorated the Holsten Gate: thistles, latticework, and lilies alternated in groups of eight, except, she was sure, for one group of seven lilies.

'You're lucky I need you alive,' Kalev said. 'But not necessarily both of you, so behave.'

55

A QUICK shout brought four guards running in. Brett and Patrick each received a preemptive punch to the gut and then had their hands bound with duct tape. With a wave, the guards were dismissed.

'Tell me how to get the dragon.' Kalev had turned to face them, his hands tucked behind his back.

'We were going to look for a series of seven lilies somewhere in here.' There was no point in lying, not in there; if they were going to get a chance to escape they'd have to move Kalev to somewhere more escapable.

'Is that all you know?'

Brett and Patrick both shrugged.

'I know where the dragon is, I just need you to open the box it's locked in.'

Dragon, singular. That was interesting. Kalev wasn't thinking beyond the next step, so she could still best him. Brett nodded. 'Okay, I'll do it.'

'Come.'

They were marched ahead of Kalev, to a room with walls clad in the same polished black stone and a single notable feature: a two-metre-square white marble box topped with a bronze sculpture. Kalev pointed towards it. 'You've got thirty minutes to open it; your friend said that you would know how.'

Brett hadn't noticed Sam until then; he was lying gagged, bound, and bleeding at the base of the marble box. She didn't much care. 'I need my hands.'

Kalev raised his gun in warning, then nodded and a guard stepped forward and cut her bonds. Brett flicked her fingers to get the circulation going and stepped over Sam to examine the sculpture.

A fantastical landscape glittered back in three dimensions. It was all seasons at once: bronze mountains climbed to peaks capped by a snow of white opals and dropped sapphire water-falls into a pool splashed by diamond foam and calmed by patches of emerald water lilies; jade pastures were dotted with wildflowers of yellow and purple topaz; while gold trees wooded the hillsides in autumnal hues; a silver dragon lorded over it all, regal in a cave midway up the mountain. 'I'll need any books or notes he had with him.'

Brett picked out the characters as she found them. Then she stepped back. Kalev looked at her. She returned his look.

The lock released with a click. Thank God.

'Stand next to him.' Kalev pointed towards Sam, and then turned to Patrick. 'You're going to help me lift this, or I'll have them both shot.'

They lifted the sculpture and laid it on the floor, revealing a hollow in the base that sparkled with warm light. As the two men stared, Brett stepped forward and plucked the dragon from its bed. Kalev grabbed her arm and drew his gun with his free hand.

'Easy, easy.' Brett pulled against his grip. 'We could share the dragons?'

Kalev jabbed her with the pistol. Brett handed over the amber sphere.

56

'WE CAN help each other out.'

Kalev looked at his audience. They looked at him. He was wearing a dark blue suit and yellow shirt open at the collar, and was smiling his awkward smile, like a fading celebrity presenting raffle prizes on a shopping mall stage. 'I have the dragons and . . .' he looked at Sam, '. . . I have the books. Now I need to know their meaning.' He spread his hands, adopting the public speaking mannerisms of a televangelist. 'So, who is going to start?'

Kalev's eyes marched from Brett to Patrick to Sam.

'Ah, perhaps I should also tell you that I have handed everything over to my cryptographers. They're very good at what they do and if they give me an answer first. . . .'

Kalev nodded to a guard, who stepped forward and ripped the tape off the prisoners' mouths, one-by-one: silence, a grunt, and a 'fuck you'. Brett almost got a slap for that, but Kalev caught the guard's raised hand and waved him away.

Kalev pulled Brett's chin upwards. 'Time's up, Brett. Talk.' He waited. 'No? No? I can make you do it, if you prefer. Or you,

Mr Moloney, our naked fighter, perhaps you'll talk to spare your pretty friend?'

'Let's make a wager of it: give me a fair fight, if you win I'll talk, if I win we go free?'

Kalev shook his head and checked his watch.

Patrick was not deterred. 'I knew it. You're scared. I'll be honest, Kalev, when I first heard that we were dealing with a Finnish mercenary, I pictured someone forged at the Helsinki Academy for Bear Wrestling or whatever; but look at you, the only bear you ever wrestled was knitted by your grandmother. So, same deal, but you leave my arms bound?'

Kalev flicked a finger and a second later, Patrick's mouth was once again covered by a strip of duct tape.

'Look, a silent Irishman.' Kalev coughed a laugh at his own joke and turned to Sam.

Just as Sam launched himself headfirst at Kalev's chest, taking everyone by surprise and knocking Kalev back a step.

The closest guard pulled Sam's arms back as a second smashed the butt of his AK-74 into his solar plexus, emptying his lungs of air and dropping Sam onto the floor. When his eyes refocused, he was on his knees with a gun barrel in his face; he sensed someone else behind him, too, no doubt just as ready to end this fight before it started, but then Kalev started to laugh. Kalev inclined his head and the guards let Sam go. They didn't holster their guns, though.

Kalev shrugged off his jacket, undid the second-from-the-top button of his shirt, rolled up his sleeves, and dropped two gold cufflinks into a guard's open hand. He beckoned Sam closer. The smile that stretched Kalev's face was the first genuinely happy one they'd seen from him.

The two guards in front of Sam stepped apart while a third kicked him forward. Sam jumped up as Kalev approached with raised fists. The two combatants circled each other like bristling wolves. Kalev feinted and laughed as Sam flinched, then threw a second, which Sam avoided. They started circling again, clockwise this time.

Sam lunged, and had to duck as Kalev counterattacked with a high left jab, and then had to step back as Kalev continued attacking with a quick right, right, left combination. Despite Patrick's taunts, Kalev clearly knew how to box. Kalev kept throwing jabs, using his longer range to keep Sam on the back foot.

Sam absorbed a flurry of blows as he forced himself closer, but used the opening to throw two quick punches of his own, a glancing blow to Kalev's ribs and a swinging left that found its mark.

It was a mistake. Kalev jerked his elbow up, catching Sam square in the face. Sam's vision blurred and his nose geysered blood. Kalev attacked with another right-left combination, and Sam retreated, until a couch blocked his way.

He was trapped.

Kalev took a step forward and threw a big haymaker.

But Sam wasn't beaten yet. He arched his spine and snapped his head back and the punch sailed high; while Kalev was still off balance, Sam replied with a kick to his unguarded kidneys. It was like striking stone.

And stone is what struck Sam a split second later, in the form of a straight right to his ribs. They might be broken, too. Sam crashed over the couch and the tinny guffaws of Kalev's men filled the room.

Kalev's arms were at his side and his cheeks were rosy. 'You actually fight quite well for an officer. Get up, I'm enjoying this.'

Sam's arms shook as he pushed himself up onto all fours, his head dangling loosely, his breath bubbling in his nose as he watched blood pool on the floor below him. Then he pounced: stayed low and tackled Kalev's knees.

Kalev's right leg crumpled.

But the tall man didn't topple. Instead, he wrapped his sinewy arms around Sam's waist and, lifting and pivoting, flung him across the room. Sam's flailing body completed a full rotation before it hit the wall, knocking loose a painting.

Sam unfolded himself in four stages while Kalev pantomimed some shadow boxing; Kalev was a cocky bastard, clearly he thought he had the fight won. When he beckoned with an open hand, Sam obliged, stepping closer, focused on Kalev's smug chin, he wound up for a final punch that he never delivered; a rifle butt struck his head from behind and Sam hit the floor unconscious.

Kalev took back his cufflinks, rolled his sleeves back down, did up the extra button, and turned to the other two. 'So, who is next?'

57

PATRICK WAS slapping the floor and grunting into his gag. Kalev nodded to a guard who ripped the duct tape off Patrick's mouth.

'Hamburg. The next dragon is in Hamburg. This can stop. You win. Well done, big guy. It only took outnumbering us by about ten to one.'

Kalev crouched, bringing himself down to Patrick's eye level. 'The thing is . . . I don't believe you. Brett was surprised when she heard your answer – she should have been angry.'

Kalev turned back to Brett and stared straight into her eyes as the guard slammed the butt of his rifle into Patrick's shoulder. She winced. A good sign. 'Where is it?'

'We don't know.' Brett's words were calm at first, and then very fast. 'Sam was the one who knew how to identify the next location and he didn't have a chance to tell us.'

Kalev gestured and the guard hit Patrick again. 'But you found that tunnel this morning without him.'

'We got lucky today, but we don't know how to find the next clue.' Once again, Patrick bore the brunt of Kalev's scepticism. 'I promise you, we don't know.' Brett was hoarse now.

'You seem tired, how about a short recess, we all have stuff to think about. I'll come and speak to each of you again shortly, perhaps you'll feel more comfortable talking in private.' Kalev waved his hand and the guards dragged Patrick, Brett, and Sam out of the room.

Brett was locked in a downstairs bathroom. It was small and although she lay contorted around the sink and toilet, it was the decor that made her wince. Fuax marble in swirls of cream and brown covered the lower half of the wall, below newer tiles in a shade of lime green.

She was miserable, but it wasn't really the tiling's fault. Her whole situation was a mess. She hadn't really noticed how far off track she was going but looking back now, this was nothing like the adventure she'd hoped for. She had wanted a challenge, but instead she had indulged herself, risking other peoples' lives and property so that she could get what she wanted.

Patrick was dumped onto the floor of an unfurnished, stale-smelling room.

It hurt even to lie still. He traced the outline of his collar-bone, seeking anomalies. Despite the pain, it appeared to be unbroken. He checked his other bruises and slowly stood. That hurt, too, but he wanted to see what lay outside the room's single window.

The view belied the ordeal they were enduring: a thriving, well laid out garden; an old oak tree was the focal point, surrounded by a lush green lawn and an undulating fringe of colourful flowers. The window was barred, heavily, and alarmed. His captors weren't stupid; if he broke the glass, he'd have mere seconds before the guards came in, not enough time to get through the bars, not even if he had a bag of tools and two uninjured arms to work with.

Having nothing better to do, he lay back on the floor and passed the time by searching for patterns in the flakes of paint that were peeling off the ceiling, like a child watching clouds.

He should never have kept Brett in this chase, he felt like a traitor now. He'd told himself that pep talk in Lübeck had been for her good, but maybe he just wanted to extend their time together or maybe, if he was one hundred percent honest with himself, he wanted more chances to show off his prowess. Brett would have walked away that day, and she would always have regretted it, he knew, but she'd be alive and that probably wouldn't be the case now.

Cold water woke Sam up. As he wiped his eyes clear, a second bucket of water hit him, and then the door was closed and locked.

He looked around, moving as little as possible. He was in a simply furnished bedroom; the blood-stained bed on which he lay was in one corner and next to it, a small bedside table held a blinking clock radio and the wall was lined with built-in wardrobes painted only in primer. He hobbled to them and looked inside. They were empty. A barred window teased him with views over the garden, but there would be no easy way out.

Sam sat back on the bed and waited.

58

HIKO NEEDED to get back to his boat to think. After a week living aboard, he couldn't think without its gentle rocking. His epidemics expert had animated a forecast of the blue dragon's rampage through London and he wanted a walk-through of the scenarios.

The epidemiologist answered on the first ring. Good, Kalev could learn from him. 'Tell me what I'm looking at.'

'The blue shading plots the predicted growth of the mould colony, the red shading shows the path of the rioting that's expected to feed off it. We've identified the perfect nursery, one block east of the target. The more we can keep the mould contained, the more violent we expect the rioting to be; and the major roads will restrict its initial spread, concentrating the effect of the rioting where you want it. Once that violence kicks off, though, well, the mould could go anywhere. The rioters will carry the spores throughout London, which, because of its damp weather and close living, is the perfect environment for it to thrive.'

'They like rioting, anyway. And drugs. So, whatever. London be damned. Just make sure the target is overwhelmed first.'

'Guaranteed. Everything is in place, except for the sample, then.'

'I'll provide the sample.'

'Or, if you don't mind me saying, sir, I could just kill her. It would be very easy to do. I could do it myself. Something untraceable. A rare disease?'

'When you were a little boy, did you ever run around in the back yard with a model aeroplane?'

'Of course, sir.'

'And when you did, did you imagine yourself as a daring pilot engaged in aerial battles, rat-a-tat-tat, shooting down the enemy?'

'Yes, sir.'

'I imagined myself as a giant, shaking the pilot's world. I hope you can understand the difference. If I only ever made sensible decisions, like killing the target easily, all I could ever become was a fighter pilot. The sample will be delivered. And then I will shake London.'

Hiko hung up. Modern medicine might be able to cure whatever throat infection the mould caused, so he was relying on a crazed mob to do his dirty work for him. He also liked the idea of his mother being trapped at her window, looking out as the chaos closed in.

Which brought him back to the mould sample: if any of it survived, it would be with the gold.

59

IT WAS dark by the time Kalev reentered the lounge. He poured himself a coffee and took a seat. The problem was not getting information – everybody talked – but in separating desperate truths from desperate lies.

He paged through the book. What Sam had said made sense, and yet it was impossible to verify without a lengthy field trip. Then again, Kalev had more time than options. He would go to Bremen. And it would be necessary to drive, given the guns he would be taking.

While a lieutenant packed the car, Kalev made sure the prisoners were secured. If he picked up the trail in Bremen, he would have someone deal with them, but if the trail was a dead end, then he would need them again. Temporarily.

Outside, the sounds of activity had died down and everything was quiet. Sam's body ached, but at least most of it still felt functional. He hobbled back to the window. Seeing the outside world helped. He wondered if the guards worked shifts, and if they did, when they changed over. That would be the best time to escape, though he assumed that he'd be dead before he had time to learn their patterns.

Wait. Was that movement in the garden? Sam concentrated on the spot: nothing, nothing, nothing, and then he saw it again, black on black, flitting between shadows, barely visible even to his alert eye.

Sam kept watching the spot, and then he threw himself to the ground.

The guards ran through the house, taking up defensive positions upstairs and downstairs, covering the prisoners' rooms, the main observation points in the master bedroom and dining room, and the fresh hole in the living room wall.

The air was dank with the citrus smell of chemicals, and brick dust, and tension.

60

ROMAN WAS holed up behind an overturned wheelbarrow. He'd filled it with sand earlier to create a one-man redoubt, though it wouldn't resist a sustained attack. He waited there for five minutes; he wanted the guards inside to get nervous before he made his move. His little bomb had worked better than expected and he felt he could afford to be a bit cocky.

Shadows moved behind the curtains, erratically enough to tell him that his plan was working. He might have risked a shot, but today he was going to have to storm the garrison alone and against the odds, so he had to wait for the right moment.

That said, he didn't want to wait long enough for backup to arrive. So, when no right moment arose, he decided to create one.

Roman tossed an orange-capped canister onto the lawn and listened to it hiss. Five. Four. The canister whined to life, spinning, whining, and spewing sparks. Three. An upstairs window shattered as gunfire tracked the canister's path. Roman pulled the trigger twice. Two. The gunman dropped dead. One. But they were good, he had signposted his location and he had to hunker down as large calibre rounds rattled his wheelbarrow. Then the canister exploded in a disorientating flash of light and noise and thick, acrid smoke.

Roman had already plotted his route and was rolling to his left before the echoes had died away, and then he was up and running, keeping low and changing direction frequently.

From a metre away, he leapt into the squat oak tree that shaded most of the garden. He climbed cautiously at first, restricted by the rate at which the smoke rose.

The random gunfire that had raked the lawn was becoming more thoughtful as visibility improved. Roman had nothing to gain by tardiness and so, using the tree as cover, he scrambled up the last five metres as fast as he could.

The branches were thinner the higher he climbed and he had to be careful as he edged towards the roof. He could almost feel them searching the garden through their rifle scopes.

Somewhere a door opened and closed and two powerful light beams began moving towards the back garden, one along the left side of the house, one along the right. They were trying to box him. He had to move. He estimated the jump from the tree to the roof. Doable. Probably. He leapt.

Roman landed awkwardly, slipping for a moment, his left arm and leg dangling over the edge. But with a silent grunt he managed to pull himself up.

He slithered along the roof, still favouring care over speed since the tiles were loose in patches. He didn't relax until he had crested the ridge, and then only a little. He scanned the front garden for threats.

Roman held onto the gutter and let his body drop onto the soft turf, rolling as he landed to dampen the impact. He rose to a crouch, pressed himself tight against the wall, and crept forward, leading with his gun. He paused at the open front door, listened, and slipped inside.

A small entrance hall opened onto rooms to his left and right, and in front of him a staircase. He went up to get the hard work out of the way first.

A passage spanned the top floor's width; Roman looked left and right and counted six identical wooden doors: three open, three closed. The gunman Roman had shot from the garden would have been in the room at the end of the passage and he hadn't been alone, so his partner was Roman's first target.

Roman ran down the passage, shoulder-charged the door, and rolled into the room as the door bounced closed behind him; a gun fired to his left, three shots in quick succession. All missed. Roman turned and fired once. The gunman dropped.

Roman dived behind the bed as the door was kicked open; he stayed crouched as footsteps padded into the room and stopped about a metre away, at his one o'clock position. He waited. Whoever had entered was waiting, too.

Then Roman heard more boots running up the stairs and gambled; trusting his ears and his luck, he sprung up, shooting. His first two shots punched massive holes in the hollow door, the third shot bore into the wall, the fourth shot knocked the man down, and the fifth shot killed him. He didn't know where the shots that had been sent his way ended up, but he was alive and the other man was not.

Three down. But the running footsteps outside had stopped and had not restarted. That made sense, they had him cornered after all. Roman's aim was trained on the shattered door, his arms extended, resting on the upturned bed, his breathing slow and calm. It was another standoff. But the two guards would be back from the garden by now; and how many others were there in the house? This was not a battle he could win by waiting.

Roman took two more pistols from his backpack and checked they were both loaded; he shoved them into his waistband and approached the door obliquely. It was closed and he would have to lean across the gaping bullet holes to open it; the man, or men, outside were no doubt waiting for him to make that mistake. He looked around the bedroom. It wasn't a room that was loved at all: an undressed bed, now upturned; a single bedside lamp, now shattered; and a free-standing wardrobe, now pockmarked.

Roman took a step back and eased the wardrobe open. It was wide and deep and home to three plain shirts and a black suit, nothing that would hide him for more than a few seconds. But *that* might be useful. Roman removed a wire coat hanger. In his hands, it quickly became a crook. Roman stood as close to the door as he dared and looped the hanger around the door handle, braced himself, and pulled.

Gunfire erupted.

Roman was giving as good as he got, and as he reloaded he tossed a stun grenade into the mêlée, aiming high. A second later he saw it flash red through his closed eyelids. That should do it. He drew one of the spare guns and rolled into the smoky passage, firing from both hands now. Roman heard a grunt to his left and concentrated on that spot, a little higher, a little lower, a little left, a little right. Then it went silent. He moved forward, slow and smooth, the gun in his right hand aimed straight ahead, the gun in his left grazing the wall to keep him on course.

He reached the nearest door without incident, and kicked it with a heel. It broke open as more gunfire sounded.

Sam was standing in front of him. Roman tossed him a gun, while shooting down the passage with the other; then he pulled the third gun from his waistband, and with Sam following in formation, edged forward once again.

Shots came at them from the end of the passage and they hit the ground. Side by side they opened fire.

A body fell and the shooting stopped.

They pushed forward again.

Roman crashed into the next door, tumbling into an unfurnished room as the lock broke, and rising to a crouch with both guns ready. Patrick's quizzical look brightened when Roman tossed him one of the guns.

It was eerie. They cleared the other rooms without encountering any resistance. Their adversaries must have sacrificed the top floor to shore up their position on the lower one.

'Any idea how many are down there?' Roman asked.

'There were eight, maybe ten men in total.' Sam looked at Patrick for confirmation. 'But they were coming and going. A car left at some stage, too. Kalev going after the treasure, I think, so with the four we downed here, it'll be roughly one-on-one from now on. Come.' Sam signalled for them to follow him down the stairs, but Roman shook his head.

'They'll be waiting for us down there, there's a better way.' He led them back to the master bedroom and, stepping over the bodies, moved to the shattered picture window. He kicked away the few glass shards that remained in the frame and pointed. 'We're going up.'

They followed Roman onto the roof and over to the front of the house. Each man checked his weapon, and aligned himself with one of the windows below: Roman above the lounge, Sam above the dining room, and Patrick above the kitchen. Roman tossed his last stun grenade over the roof and into the back garden as a diversion and, on his signal, they all dropped, opening fire as they landed.

The impact of the drop whiplashed Patrick's first volley from ceiling to floor and back again, scaring, but missing, the guard in the room, who tipped over the heavy kitchen table and took shelter behind it.

The guard fired sporadically to keep Patrick pinned behind a large tree in the front yard.
It was a stalemate.

Sam and Roman had also taken cover, having expended the element of surprise. Both men were on their stomachs, Sam peering out from under a car in the driveway and Roman from behind an ornamental water feature. They were patient because they had the advantage; although the guards had killed the living room lights, it was still brighter inside the house than outside, making the front window a one-way mirror.
Roman crawled to a better shooting position and gave Sam the signal. They squeezed their triggers simultaneously and two guards in the lounge dropped. A third guard sprinted for cover in the passage while his colleague in the kitchen took the opportunity to run, too, though Patrick tripped him with a shot to his trailing leg.
Breathing heavily, Patrick, Sam, and Roman converged on the front door.

61

MATTHYS FIDGETED, waiting for the opportunity to ease his news into the conversation. He couldn't stop smiling, though; he had a real lead and actual physical evidence. Of course, what he didn't have was the briefing paper for the upcoming conference on intra-Europe police cooperation, which was why he was so cautious about how he spoke.

There were three things about the phone calls from Hong Kong that excited him: one, they started two days after St George was last spotted in Paris; two, they started before the other phones clustered together; and, three, although the phone in Hong Kong wasn't used often, it was the only one that had called both the first and second teams. Matthys wasn't so naïve as to think that his superior officers would infer anything more substantial than a link between the wreck gang and someone in Hong Kong, but he knew those calls proved the existence of St George.

Anyway, if there were three independent art thieves operating in Europe, then why did they all go quiet the moment he tracked St George to Paris? And why did these dragon-related calls start two days later in Hong Kong? Coincidences didn't come this big in the real world. He knew what he needed to do; it was a simple branding problem.

He would pitch it as a project to assist on that wreck case, rather than as a way to catch St George – which would also save him from having to explain why he was still working a case that had officially been closed for a week and instead leverage one with actual traction.

Matthys also had to decide whether to mention the fact that he had already spoken to the police in Hong Kong.

62

'BRETT, I'M sorry I had to do what I did to you back in Tallinn, but now at least you can see what we're up against.' Sam waved vaguely at his bashed and bloody face. 'This is what I was trying to protect you from.'

'No – you wanted to keep me from the gold, not protect me from "this".' She mimicked his flourish.

'That's not fair, Brett.'

'Sam, shut up. If you try to lecture me on what is and isn't fair I'll punch you, too.'

'I'm sorry. I was trying to protect you. I'm a soldier and that's what we do.'

'So, you're the big strong man that protected the defenceless little girl?'

'Brett, it's not like that, it's. . . . Ah, I'm sorry. Okay?'

'We need to get going. Unless you'd rather stay here and protect these dishes?'

'Brett.'

'Sam, how about I say that I accept that you acted in good faith, and you just shut up and help me stop Kalev.'

'Don't be like that, I'm the reason we even have a chance.'

After a savage beating Sam had conceded defeat. He had showed Kalev how to arrange the pages to form a map of Bremen; he had pointed out the embossed cross; he had shown him how to use the last amber sphere to select the right key; and he had even placed the key over the cross and shown him how it circled St Stephen's Church. Then Sam had collapsed.

He deserved an Oscar for that. Actually being quite badly hurt helped the performance, of course.

The car had left about thirty minutes later, which meant that Kalev had a two-hour head start. He also had the dragons and the books. Fortunately for them, he was going to the wrong place. So now, if they moved quickly, they might catch up with him while he was still in Bremen.

Kalev was going to take the dragons regardless; the only thing Sam could do was control where he took them. Sam had told him everything except that he had to flip the key into the white space.

The previous day, Roman had woken feeling hung over and annoyed; not one for being mollycoddled, he had called Sam to get back in the action, but Sam hadn't answered. When Roman's calls and messages remained unanswered for six hours, Roman traced Sam to the old farmhouse using an application loaded onto the phone Sam had borrowed from him in Riga.

Eight hours after that, Roman was in the garden with a bag full of guns and grenades.

And now they were all in Roman's Ford Focus, cleaned and serviced since its excursion through Latvian fields, thundering along the autobahn. Roman was driving, Sam was in the passenger seat, Brett and Patrick were in the back. Roman had even turned down the music, a little, to allow them to hold a shouted conversation.

'I think we should go in two teams of two, one through the main door and one through this side door near the altar.' Sam held a floor plan of the church under the interior light. St Stephen's Church had been built in 1139 and was once an important place of worship, now it acted as a cultural centre and venue for the arts. 'We'll take him by surprise and maximise our chances.'

'There's no way we're splitting up,' Brett said. 'We also don't know how many men he has with him, so we'll need all four of us to stand a chance.'

'She's right,' Patrick said.

'Okay, frontal assault. Through the main door?' Roman was making a worrying amount of eye contact given the speed at which he was driving.

'I think we should be more subtle about it,' Patrick said. 'Let's all go in the main door, but let's slip in, not barge in.' He looked around, the others were nodding. 'Sam and I'll go in first, Roman, you bring up the rear, and the rest we make up as we go along?'

'Sounds like my kind of plan,' Roman said, as he bumped up the volume.

They coasted around the last few bends with the headlights off, coming to a stop 300 metres from the church.

It looked dark and empty, as it should at that time of night. The team spread out and followed Patrick towards the front door. It was unlocked, and a gentle push opened it with a smooth and silent motion. Patrick peered inside. Seeing no obvious danger, he beckoned them closer and eased through the half-opened door.

Large metal shapes that would have been called 'offcuts' in an industrial setting stood on pedestals and were now called 'art'. Patrick allowed his eyes to adjust to the gloom, and then padded around the first exhibit – rusty pipes twisted into a shape that vaguely resembled a cube. He dived straight back as a shot rang out and its extremities shattered into no less artistic pieces. The others hit the ground, too, taking cover wherever they could.

Patrick drew his gun and crawled beyond the cube. Someone had spotted him. But who? And from where? He scanned the dark room, hoping the sound of the others shuffling behind him might tempt the gunman to betray his location. He saw nothing, so he crawled back behind the sculpture, rose, and sprinted to the next one – a series of tubing spirals meshed together without any obvious foresight. No more shots came.

Patrick spun around.

Sam pointed to himself and to their left, and then to Patrick and to the right. Patrick nodded, held up five fingers, and then dropped them in a steady countdown. On cue they both ran.

Their footsteps slapped on the stone floor, loud until the sound of gunfire drowned them out. Bullets flew past Patrick, coming from a disorientating array of directions, cracking around his feet, sparking against sculptures, and shattering stained-glass windows high along on the far wall. The sculpture he was running towards was still fifteen metres away and all he could do was keep his head down and hope that the fact they were in a church would somehow protect him.

Sam saw three metal ribbons rising two metres from the ground and twisting themselves around each other in a loose bow. He was halfway to this misshapen refuge when the shooting restarted. He was too exposed to risk making himself a well-lit target, so he held his fire and kept running.

Roman and Brett were running to the sculpture that Sam and Patrick had just left, when the shots came. Roman pulled Brett to the ground and drew his gun.

He scanned the room. Guns flashed erratically across the room, but they were not aiming at them.

Roman helped Brett back to her feet and shepherded her forward. Once they'd reached relative safety in the lee of the sculpture, he fired a fan of six shots, covering as best he could the area from which enemy fire had originated. He dropped back out of sight and reloaded as bullets screamed in angry rebuttal.

And just as suddenly, the room went silent.

When the shooting started again, it was evangelical in volume. Choruses of shots sang from the chancel and windows shattered, shards fell to the stone floor.

Patrick stopped shooting as window after window came down. He had also stopped being shot at, which was significant. He looked at Sam, standing ten metres away, equally still. 'We need to get out of here. Now!'

63

Patrick was staring at a dozen serious-faced men. They had guns, too, and theirs were much bigger than his and aimed at him. Patrick raised his arms and submitted to a rough pat down.

The police yelled out for calm, and took Sam, Roman, and Brett into custody. Kalev's timing had been superb; his little charade had clearly roused the police, but not before he'd slipped their net leaving four fools to answer their questions.

'May I make a phone call?' Patrick asked the guard outside his cell.

'This isn't the movies,' the policeman replied.

'Of course, but perhaps you could take my wallet from the evidence locker and hand it to your boss. I'm sure that if you show him my ID he'd appreciate it.'

That they were back on the road now was entirely due to Patrick's phone call, though he refused to say what had been discussed or with whom. They were back on the road, he pointed out, and that was all that mattered.

Roman shifted into fifth gear, engaged the turbo, and threw them past a family sedan.

They were going to Dötlingen, a small hamlet forty kilometres southwest of Bremen. It hadn't taken them long to come to that decision. When Sam had told Kalev to find St Stephen's, he had kept an eye open for the real location of the clue. Without the key it was something of a guess, but in the end Dötlingen was the only viable option, surrounded as it was by farms and forest reserves for several kilometres in each direction. If they could jump ahead of Kalev there, they'd be back in the game.

After ten minutes, Roman lowered the volume. 'We've got a tail. I think. Or I could be paranoid.'

'The police again? Patrick?' Sam asked. He had been brooding since the chaos in the church.

'Don't you get so huffy,' Brett said. 'If Patrick had listened to me, we'd have left you in the cell.'

'And if you had listened to my advice, we'd all be drinking a beer somewhere safe,' Patrick said.

'We've spoken about this, but you're more than welcome to take Sam for that drink if you both want out.'

'I don't think it's the police,' Roman said, playing peace broker. 'It's two cars working together, a silver Audi about ten cars back, in the middle lane, and the red Mercedes that's ahead of us now in the right lane, behind that truck. I'll get us closer.'

'Don't look. Don't look,' Roman added like an infatuated teenager. But everyone did: it was Kalev.

And Kalev had spotted them, too. He accelerated and swung the Mercedes into their lane, then jumped on his brakes, forcing Roman to do the same. The silver Audi grew in the rearview mirror, boxing them in. Roman looked for an opening, but cars raced past on their left and right now. Roman dropped the car into third gear and hit the accelerator; he would have to make his own gap.

Tyres squealed, spun, and gripped as he fishtailed in front of the protesting traffic and passed Kalev again. Roman ignored the painted lanes, shooting between two cars to get to an open stretch of road, his foot unforgiving. In his mirror he saw the other two bullying their way through the crowd. 'Don't worry, I can lose them,' Roman said. 'But I need the music back.'

'No, don't lose them. The fish are biting again, better to string them along,' Brett said from the back.

'I can outrun him, you know that, right?'

'No one is saying you can't, big guy. He has what we need, though, and right now he's bringing it to us.'

Brett was leaning forward, her hands squeezing Roman's shoulders as if he were a prizefighter.

There was a moment of silence in the car before Roman gave the accelerator the smallest respite.

'Why don't we call your friends and ask for some police backup?' Sam asked from the front seat.

'I told you, that was a once-off. Someone owed me a favour and now they don't. The police aren't our friends.'

Sam grunted and stretched out a roadmap. 'Don't let him catch you, either.'

'Oh, there's no chance of that.'

Roman took the off-ramp and the road immediately wandered into the Wildeshauser Geest Nature Reserve that surrounded Dötlingen; he checked his mirrors and saw Kalev take the same exit. The gap was closing. But Brett urged him to stay slow.

The Mercedes ballooned in his mirror, showing no signs of similar restraint.

'He's going to pass, let—' Brett was cut off by the crash. Seat belts snapped taut and metal bent as Kalev hit them at high speed. He clearly had a different plan.

Roman muscled the Ford straight and hit the accelerator. The Mercedes still filled all of his mirrors, with three views of Kalev's anger. The two cars were inches apart now, maintaining the status quo at a 160 kilometres per hour.

Sam drew his gun, but kept it out of view, spinning in his seat to watch the chase; the fingers on his other hand dancing along the handbrake.

Dötlingen was five kilometres away. Roman wasn't even sitting any more as he stood on the accelerator and fought for more speed.

Then Kalev hit them again. He clipped the Ford's back right corner and the car started to slide, before Roman corrected it. Kalev hit them again.

This time, Sam pulled up the handbrake and Roman spun the wheel. The rear of the car swung around in a half circle of squealing smoke and Kalev flew past. Roman accelerated towards the silver Audi, which had been a spectator until now. The driver panicked; he slammed on the brakes and stalled the engine as he tried to avoid the maniacal Ford.

Sam repeated the handbrake spin and they were facing Kalev again, and he was reversing towards them. Roman shot forward. He didn't care about the Audi anymore; this was between them and Kalev. Roman bounced on the accelerator and jabbed through the gears. Kalev wasn't backing down, either. They were a hundred metres apart. Fifty. Ten.

Kalev assumed that they were trying to evade him again, so when Roman jagged right, Kalev moved to block him, but Roman straightened and swung hard into the Mercedes' back corner. The impact amplified the Mercedes' own momentum, spinning it around two and a half rotations and cracking its rear axle.

The Ford swayed, bumped over the verge, and bit into the soft earth before Roman hauled it back onto the blacktop; its left headlight and front bumper had suffered under the impact, adding pebbles of white glass and black paint to the chaotic fallout, but the engine was still running. Behind them, Kalev was climbing out of the crippled Mercedes and flagging down the Audi.

64

ROMAN DIDN'T slow down when they entered Dötlingen; any thoughts of remaining unobtrusive were foiled in any case by the Ford's dented visage and smoking brakes. Dötlingen was a charming location for a showdown: a hamlet of picturesque stone buildings placed around a village green and the bleached trunk of a thousand-year-old oak tree that shone like ivory at its centre.

They abandoned the Ford and ran back towards the main road. Kalev could be no more than a minute behind.

It was less. The silver Audi was already storming towards the ambush site when they reached it.

'Positions!' Sam's grumpiness evaporated as soon as the action started.

Brett and Patrick dived into a roadside drainage ditch, Roman ran across the road trailing two tracks of heavy-duty spikes, and Sam watched to make sure everything went to plan. When Roman reached the other side of the road, he dropped into a shooting stance and gave Sam a thumbs up. Sam replied with the same, and mirrored his stance, both of their guns trained on the fast-approaching vehicle.

It wasn't slowing down.

They were holding their fire.

And then the Audi's windscreen exploded. Two fist-sized holes burst through the glass as the passenger fired. Two more booming shots followed. Sam and Roman hunched as buckshot cratered the road in front, between, and behind them, but they held their positions.

The car was less than twenty metres away when they pulled their triggers. The Audi's passenger fired at the same time and for a slow second, the air was saturated with bullets. A perforation of holes raced along the car's bonnet, up the windscreen, and beyond. A second line started as sparks on the left wheel arch and ended as a cluster of holes in the driver's door. The buckshot's trajectory was less easy to trace. Sam stood firm as dirt and tarmac danced around him. Roman was less lucky. The second shot struck him square in the shoulder, punching him back onto the soft earth.

The car kept coming.

Sam emptied another magazine. The passenger discharged both barrels. And Kalev failed to see the spikes that Roman had left in the road. The tyres burst and spun to shreds, lurching the Audi into a screeching collision course with Sam. Sam tracked its progress, reloaded with practised speed, fired eight times, and dived out of the way.

Just in time.

The Audi's bare wheels cut anchoring trenches in the soft ground, slowing it down while its momentum urged it forward, flipping it up and over and over and over.

When it came to rest, the Audi was on its roof with its wheels turning unevenly.

Sam jumped up and ran towards the wreck with his gun drawn. Patrick approached from the driver's side. Brett ignored them both and ran to check on Roman.

Roman was lying in a bloody puddle where he'd fallen, his skin was cool to the touch and pale against the black and scarlet backdrop. His eyes were unresponsive.

Brett rummaged through his messy backpack, finding everything except a first aid kit. There was a bottle of vodka though, so it could have been worse. Brett forced a reviving drop through Roman's lips and watched his chest; if that didn't revive Roman, she didn't know what would.

Sam and Patrick edged closer. The only thing moving in the wrecked car was a geyser of foul-smelling steam that hissed through a crack in the dashboard, the only sound was the wail of damaged metal as it settled into its new shape.

The interior of the car was in turmoil, its contents shuffled and dealt at random across the overturned roof; its occupants hanging upside down in their seats, blood running down both their impassive faces.

Patrick knelt next to the driver's door and nudged Kalev's head with the barrel of his gun. It swayed gently. He leaned in and held two fingers to Kalev's throat; Kalev was alive. A pity, but killing a man in battle was very different to killing an unconscious man in cold blood, so Patrick left him. And anyway, Patrick could see the green duffle bag they were looking for.

The rear window had shattered in the crash, so he kicked away the last jagged shards and stretched through the buckled frame to retrieve it, along with the stolen dragons inside.

Sam yanked open the passenger door and dropped to his knees to look inside. The other man was shorter than Kalev, but not by much, and he was considerably bulkier; his square jaw and broad forehead suggested Teutonic roots. A local hire, perhaps.

Sam was looking for the shotgun. He saw it among the detritus and slid into the car to grab it. Its barrel was warm, heavy and unadorned, an efficient weapon with none of the redeeming charm of the heirloom he'd inherited from his grandfather. It would have to do.

65

THE DUFFLE bag had snagged on something in the deformed interior so Patrick wriggled further in, head-first and on his back like a mechanic, though this car would never run again.

The bag's strap had wrapped around the handbrake and Patrick unwound it, once clockwise, then once anticlockwise. But a sharp elbow to the side of his head stopped him before he could drag it free. Kalev was still suspended by his seat belt, but he was wide awake now and fighting.

Kalev's hands swung back and forth, snapping like painted hunting dogs, and caught Patrick's collar. Kalev twisted in his seat, throwing awkward punches with his left hand while he held Patrick in place with his right. Patrick chose not to block the blows. Instead, he tried to back out the car, jerking his body in an attempt to loosen Kalev's grip. But Kalev held firm.

The shotgun exploded. Its vibrating barrel burned Sam's hands but he never flinched. And again.

Sam tried to force an opportunity, risking a single-handed grip as he rammed his forearm into the tangled passenger's head. It was an ineffective blow and the passenger wrenched the gun back, pulling Sam forward with it. Sam never lost his grip – to do so would be fatal.

Sam swung his right arm again, landing two solid blows this time and winning an inch in the tug-of-war. Then he was struck himself, with a fist to the bridge of his nose. Sam's head snapped back; using the extra leverage, and the muscles in his stomach and neck, he swung it forward with interest and head-butted the man's chin.

Kalev now had Patrick wrapped in an upside down bear hug. Kalev's uncomfortable position kept him from applying sufficient power to squeeze Patrick into unconsciousness, but with Patrick struggling to find traction in the scree of broken glass that littered the overturned wreck, it was enough to keep him from escaping.

Patrick regretted his earlier taunts.

Their sweating, bleeding faces were mere centimetres apart.

Patrick's legs were still free, though, so he drew his knees into his abdomen and kicked upwards. His first kick hit the top of Kalev's head, the next two struck Kalev's forearms. As Patrick's fourth kick landed, he jerked his arms away from his body and thrashed his torso, finally breaking Kalev's grip. Patrick immediately rolled deeper into the car, evading Kalev, who had lunged the other way. Seeing his opportunity, Patrick smashed a pointed elbow into Kalev's exposed throat and released the seatbelt, dropping Kalev onto his head.

Patrick unhooked the duffle bag and rolled out the rear window just as Sam staggered out the front one, carrying a shotgun.

66

BRETT LEVERED Roman into a sitting position.

She slapped his cheeks to no reaction, so she eased a drop of vodka through Roman's split lips. Although his eyes popped open, they remained blank and uninterested. They certainly didn't register Sam and Patrick when they arrived but, then again, Brett was ignoring them, too. She fed Roman a second capful.

'No, stop. That's awful.' Roman swallowed and blinked as the vodka retouched his complexion. 'Why did you give me that?'

'I'm sorry, I thought—'

He licked his lips. 'There's a small bottle of Stoli Elit in there somewhere, and don't be shy, I stole it from the First Class galley on my last flight; that other stuff is just for cleaning wounds. It's Swedish.' Then he broke into a broad smile. It looked like the second time that week he would be shot and survive.

'Are you okay?' Brett asked.

'Perfect. As usual.' He scratched at the last cotton strands of his torn shirt. Underneath, he wore a blue Kevlar vest, across which a constellation of flattened silver disks mapped the mortal damage that he might otherwise have incurred. 'I'm just not sure if I can stand on my own yet.'

Brett helped him up. 'I think you should rest for a bit, though, we can wait.'

'No, we can't, and no doctor's going to be babysitting me this time. I'm fine. Let's go.' Roman hobbled five steps ahead, then stopped and turned around, 'Where are we going?'

A neat grid of wooden cottages grew outwards from Dötlingen's village green, borrowing shade from the ancient linden trees that grew almost as densely in their gardens as the pines did in the forest. St Firmin's Church was at the very edge of the village, on a hill and serenaded by a gentle stream.

It was a child's drawing of a church. A straight-profiled roof sat atop walls that appeared light pink from afar, but which were in fact a fusion of red and grey fieldstone held together by thick white mortar. The short tower was decorated with the church's only embellishment: a cobalt blue clock whose gold hands caught the afternoon sun.

They walked straight to the front door, which was heavy but unlocked. Sam pulled it open.

Sunlight streamed in through high windows, gilding two low hanging chandeliers and warming a dozen rows of straight-backed pews. Roman took a seat and used a sponge of holy water to clean his wounds, not because he was a religious man; in fact, probably only because he wasn't. The others explored the interior.

Vaulted ceilings, ribbed in grey and pink, divided the small church into three clear sections, and they spread out to search each simultaneously. But one by silent one, they congregated at the same spot, all drawn to the stained glass window above the main door; the red, yellow, and blue light it threw bounced like tossed dice on the flagstone floor. It was Sam again who broke the silence, giving an excited voice to the thought on everyone's lips. 'This can't be a coincidence.'

A winged angel, robed in gold, stood with a spear thrust into a vanquished dragon.

Leaving Roman to rest, a reenergised Patrick, Brett, and Sam resumed the search for the amber globe. Patrick searched the pews first, recalling the little mice Robert Thompson had playfully carved into church furniture across Britain, and hoping to find a similar sign here; these pews, though, were designed for a more puritan form of worshiper and were bare. The floor was thoroughly plain, too. Nonetheless, he took up the fool's task of walking and tapping, walking and tapping, listening for a hollowness in the tone.

Brett walked to the organ. Though silent now, it turned her mind to memories of Sunday school and poor little Nino Rossi, whose mother pushed him to flout peer pressure and sparse talent to make a joyful noise unto the Lord. It was an awe-inspiring piece of furniture, carved with scenes of harvest, scenes of worship, and scenes from Christ's life story. Brett crawled and stretched, but found nothing unusual.

Sam examined the paintings, looking for symbolism among the religious iconography.

'Patrick, stop,' Brett shouted from across the church. 'Now take a step left.'

'Here?'

'No, sorry, my left. A little more. Now come two steps towards me.'

'What's going on?' Sam had stopped his search to watch. 'Have you found it?'

Brett had seen it when she turned back from the organ: the stained glass window's message glowing bright in its recessed frame.

They'd all focused on the angelic dragon-slayer, but the surrounding trim was where the message lay. The window was bordered by small rectangles, neatly divided into three sections by bolder lines, two rectangular and one semicircular: the rectangles were seven stones wide and four stones long, the semicircle was twelve stones around the top. Just like the floor plan of the church.

If she was right, and it made perfect sense to her now, the spot the angel's spear was pointing to would be the spot that they were looking for.

'I think we need to dig right where Patrick is standing now.'

'You sure?'

'No, I'm not sure. Just help him dig and stop looking for reasons to moan.'

Sam fetched a hammer and a crowbar and together, he and Patrick began to defile the church.

Kalev sat on the grass, with his knees pulled up to his chest and his forehead resting on them. He was sucking in deep breaths and assessing his injuries: nothing too serious. The harsh smell of spilled petrol helped to revive his senses. He looked across at the car where his colleague still hung, out cold. He had to decide what to do about him.

Kalev fumbled in his jacket pockets until he came back with a buckled pack of cigarettes. He tapped them all out, discarded the broken ones, lit one of the straightest survivors, and sucked on it; then he approached the car.

The air still stank of the crash. Kalev took a deep drag, then shook the dented boot open. In their haste, the others had missed the handguns hidden in the wheel well. A second shooter could come in handy. Kalev stamped out his cigarette and pulled the man free.

67

'YOU CAME to me claiming friendship, Chief Inspector Rossouw, but you've disregarded all established protocols and you've made a lot of trouble for me.'

Matthys wasn't actually a Chief Inspector, but he wasn't going to point it out to a man who was the same age as he was and two full rungs higher up on the career ladder. Matthys examined Gu's features as he spoke. He was very good looking, in the clean-cut sort of way that usually came from a strict but prosperous upbringing. Matthys noticed a change in the volume of the conversation and focused on Gu's words again.

'What you're proposing was not discussed when my superiors signed off on this mission.'

The air outside was steamy and a little grey. Inside it was just steamy. Chief Inspector Gu's face gave the room colour enough. He was almost apoplectic. That annoyed Matthys a little. Sure, Matthys was strong-arming the man into helping him, but how else did a cop get things done?

Matthys looked out the window. The headquarters of the Hong Kong Police Force enjoyed an enviable location beside the harbour, but he noted that Gu had been relegated to a room that overlooked a parking lot. Expenses had been spared when decorating it, too; the walls were unadorned and three previous desk locations were fossilised in the threadbare carpet.

'Now, I can either support your foolish plan or risk a political fracas. I don't appreciate being put in that position. I have no option but to give you permission to continue your investigation in my city, so I will, for a week. A week, Mr Rossouw, and no more. Thereafter, you either need to be back in Holland or show me real evidence I can act on.'

Now he was just a mister. Oh well. 'Thank you, Chief Inspector. And could I have a dozen local officers as backup?'

'Who do you think you. . .!' Chief Inspector Gu pinched the bridge of his nose and watched Matthys stand and turn for the door.

Gu exhaled. 'Wait, Chief Inspector. I cannot waste police resources on a junket, but if you show me that a dangerous criminal is operating in my city, I will bring him to justice. So I'll brief six men in my command. Any leads you uncover are to be routed through me and then I'll decide if and when my men are deployed. You are not to engage the suspect. Do you understand?'

Matthys nodded and left. He had been in Hong Kong for twelve hours and already he was making progress.

68

THE FLAGSTONE succumbed to the dual assault, chipping into thin flakes at first, and then splitting into six roughly equal segments as the chisel broke through, gonging into something metal below. Patrick and Sam quickly lifted the pieces away, revealing the now-familiar patina of old bronze. They wiped away the dust, revealing a copy of the scene from the window.

Brett dropped beside him. 'I had thought we'd be looking for a lion, but I can see at least six of them.' Brett raised her brows at the other two. 'Ideas?'

The symbols were arranged more precisely than they had been before: starting in the middle of the disk's top edge, they spiralled inwards until a final dragon rested under the point of the angel's spear.

Sam fetched the book and joined them on the floor. 'Do you mind if I have a quick look at the code first?'

'Go ahead.' Brett's tone was neutral.

He read the story quickly, nodding to himself while saying nothing.

'Well?'

'Well, what would you do if, dare I say it, you were hiding the actual treasure?'

'Just tell us!' Roman called from his pew, pushing himself up onto an elbow. The holy water must have done him some good.

'Well, I'd make sure that someone couldn't get lucky and just stumble onto the final hiding place; and one way to do that would be by using all of the clues from start to finish. Look, the last symbol in the Bremen story is a dragon and there it is, right there. X marks the spot. So, extrapolating the logic backwards, we should start with the first symbol you used in Tallinn.'

'No,' Brett said. 'We should start with what would have been the first symbol in . . . Visby, hopefully. Do we agree that that's where the *Drachen* was most likely headed when it sunk?'

No one agreed, no one disagreed.

'Thanks for the help, guys.' Brett turned to the Visby page.

Kalev jogged with the uneven gait of a hyena that smelled a kill. The stocky man limping beside him looked even more terrifying than Kalev did, with a duct-taped gash splitting his cheek and two dark bruises underlining his eyes.

Both men had their guns drawn.

The church of St Firmin appeared between the trees, perched on a small rise on the other side of a pebbled stream. They had circled the building to evade detection and were approaching from the far side. No sentries had been posted outside, though. Perhaps that was because they weren't needed; the high windows offered great shooting positions to any defenders.

Kalev had to risk it.

They jumped across the stream and broke cover at a full sprint. Halfway up the hill, an alarm gonged from within the church. The two men hit the ground with their weapons raised. But no shots came. Kalev scanned the windows and saw no movement, so they were up again and running.

Still no shots came.

They split up when they reached the church's wall and started to circle the building. If they were going to walk into another ambush, they would at least make it difficult.

A minute later, Kalev dropped onto his knees and, leading with his weapon, peered around the corner. He nodded, and the two men converged on the church's main door, hanging half ajar.

That would be where they were most at risk. It was the perfect killing field. But this wasn't their first assault, either. With professional synchronicity, Kalev dived in as his colleague booted the door fully open. He rolled and rose into a shooting stance, protected by the fast arc of his gun, and the fact that the church was empty.

Patrick was first down the narrow staircase, followed by Brett, and then Roman. Sam covered their rear, watching the church as the echo of their footsteps receded. When no one came, he followed them down.

The staircase coiled around a deep, black drop and Sam trailed his fingers along the rough wall as he descended, leaning slightly away from the drop. He was in his own world, thinking about what they might find. Could this really be where the *Drachen's* treasure lay?

A sound brought him back to reality.

Though now he was listening, it was silent again. The sound could have come from any direction, even from within his imagination. Sam waited. His nerves tingled. Nothing happened.

Kalev strode towards the hole in the broken floor and listened. It was quiet. He looked down. And empty. He stepped back and gently straightened his last cigarette. 'Give them five minutes. The winner in this game will be the one who ends with the treasure, not the one who gets there first.'

When they followed, it was with their left hands carrying guns and their right hands tracing the curve of the wall as it twisted downwards.

69

THE STAIRS ended in a room humming with volatile chatter. Brett silently pointed out the problem: her headlamp illuminated a gap-toothed wooden bridge, suspended, such as it was, from the ceiling on the dozen leather hangers that had not yet dried and cracked. Though many more had. Even in the windless space, it swung on its uneven supports. The rope that was supposed to act as a handrail lay useless across the remaining wooden planks.

The place they needed to get to, the next piece of solid rock, was forty metres away, across a deep crevasse.

Sam looked at Roman, then at Patrick, and finally at Brett, who refused to lift her gaze to meet his. 'Are you sure we can't do it another way? Couldn't we climb down? I'm not sure I trust that, ah, construction.'

Brett scuffed her feet and clenched her fists.

Patrick put an arm around her shoulders and gave her a squeeze, then turned to Sam. 'No, we have fifty metres of climbing rope and this hole is deeper than that. And then we'd still have to get up the other side.'

Sam stepped forward, looking back and forth between the bridge and his colleagues. 'On the plus side, I guess, is that it is still standing. . . .'

'Just.' Roman added with a thin smile. 'But we think that there might be a way around it. Look at the leather hangers, they've decayed of course, but look there, where they were connected to the roof, those look like stone Samson posts and they won't have deteriorated. If we can get our rope around one near the middle, we could swing across.'

'And how do we reach it?' Sam asked. 'That's pretty long walk on a pretty flimsy bridge.'

'Yeah, that's the reason our beautiful friend here has turned green: I'll have to walk out. Maybe not as far as halfway, but most of the way there.'

Sam shook his head. 'The hell you will. Even if you manage to hook one of those posts you'll still need to climb up to the roof to put in some proper bolts before we can use it as a swing; your shoulder couldn't take that. I'll go first.'

'Wait—'

Sam raised a hand to cut Roman off. 'This isn't altruism; you owe me a bottle of vodka if this ends badly. The bloody good stuff, too. And be ready to catch me if that bridge collapses.' Sam turned and spoke to Brett. 'Once I'm across I'll bolt the rope to something on that side to create a stable pendulum. Patrick will help you into a climbing harness so when you swing there's no risk of you falling. It's not a lie-flat bed and champagne, but it's as close to first class as I can offer. You won't be at risk.'

'I'm not fucking swinging!' Brett still didn't look up.

'Only if the bridge collapses, in which case it'll be better than jumping.' Sam stepped forward and placed one foot on the bridge, pressing down slightly to test it. Now his heart was beating faster as the bridge creaked and bounced. He took a deep breath. And put his second foot on the bridge, assuming a wide, waddling stance as he edged forward.

Although the wooden planks bent underfoot, they supported his weight, but after just ten steps a leather support snapped in a puff of dust.

When a second hanger snapped, Sam stopped. He was still a long way from the middle, but he lined up his throw. His first three attempts didn't come close, which he took as a sign he'd need to get closer. But when another hanger snapped on his very next step, he focused on steadily improving his aim.

He'd looped the rope through a rotor swivel to create a small lasso. That was the extent to which technique played a role, from there on out he relied on luck. Sam swung the weighted rope in fast circles, releasing it at the top of its arc with a flick of his wrist and a prayer.

But it worked, on his twentieth attempt. Sam leant back and allowed the noose to slowly tighten around the chiselled rock peg.

Now was the moment of truth. Sam gave the rope a sharp tug. Since it didn't come loose, he jerked it again. And again. Satisfied, he walked forward until he was directly underneath the pivot point. Sam connected a Tibloc ascender to the rope and hauled himself upwards.

It was hard work. But once he'd reached the ceiling, bolted two heavy-duty pulleys in place, and wound the rope through them, he knew his job was as good as done. At least until they reached the other side. Who knew what lay there.

Sam slid back down the rope, touching down as gently as possible. Despite now having a safety line, he desperately wanted to make it across on foot. While the doubling-up of pulleys did provide an extra level of safety, the primary reason for this array was to allow someone on the far bank to pull in a swinging passenger.

The bridge swayed, and a piece of wood dropped off. He slid another step forward. And another, and another, until his feet found solid rock. Sam tied his backpack to the rope and swung it back to the others.

True to her word, Brett didn't swing, she skipped across the bridge with the grace of a dancer. Though by the time she reached Sam, the bridge was in a precarious condition: more than half of the planks had disintegrated, and only two of the leather hangers were still in place, one on either side of the bridge.

Roman went next. He chose to run. And for his first dozen steps it worked. And then it didn't. So rotted was the plank he landed on that it didn't so much snap as crumble. Roman fell straight through it, grabbing instinctively for support, but bringing down the bridge instead.

It collapsed in a single continuous process that raced away from him in both directions as the final strands snapped, and Roman was swinging towards the wall. Sam hauled in the climbing rope to steepen Roman's arc, while Brett cleared the rope as it piled behind him.

It was a hell of a ride. Roman was flying towards them, coming in from below but gaining height all the way. Was it enough height, though?

Just. Roman landed next to them with a whoop.

And a minute later they were watching Patrick prepare to make the crossing.

70

KALEV WAVED his lieutenant closer and together they slipped into the room. Almost too late.

He aimed and fired at the flying headlamp. The burst was echoed on his left. And then the room went dark.

The two men retreated as return fire sparkled across the divide, but the image that repeated with every blink of his eyes warmed Kalev's heart: the curly-haired Irishman falling into the abyss.

Roman reloaded and fired a slow beat of covering fire, taking six steps left and six steps right to create the illusion of multiple shooters. Behind him, Brett and Sam worked in unison, hauling in the rope and clearing it, hauling in the rope and clearing it, pulling Patrick in.

They had seen Kalev just as Patrick had started his run up, they had seen him fire as Patrick leapt, and had seen Patrick fall.

'It's a weak opponent who worries more about a corpse than the battle.' Kalev strode back into the room and stood among the scattered shots. They were firing from too far away to be of any danger to him. He walked closer to the crevasse and stared downwards, trying to follow the path of the weighted rope as it disappeared from view.

He chose his mark, and fired.

The rope vibrated, then went still; then he raked the far bank with gunfire for a laugh.

'Brett, we need to leave him.'

'Leave him? He might be alive, you bastard!' Brett had grabbed fistfuls of Sam's shirt and was screaming into his too-calm face. 'We can't just leave him.'

'We must, Brett. Right now we're making him a target.'

'You're just peddling the same old bullshit, aren't you? It's for his own good, it's for my own good, and yet it's always you that's getting closer to the treasure.'

'I'm not, Brett. You saw what happened. If we stick around they'll keep shooting at him to get at us. They don't care about him, he's no threat to them anymore, they want the dragons; and the sooner we draw them into the tunnel, the sooner they'll leave him be. We need to be rational here.'

'I don't care how you rationalise abandoning a friend, but I won't do it.'

'I was in Sarajevo, Brett, during the siege. I lost someone I cared about to a sniper there, she was hiding, waiting it out, but the sniper never went away. I should have, I mean if I could have, you know, drawn the fire, then maybe. . . . What I'm saying is that we're not leaving him behind. We will come back for him as soon as we can. I promise you that.'

'We'll find somewhere to stage an ambush and at three against two, we'll have the numerical advantage. Then we can return to get Patrick,' Roman added.

Brett wasn't sure if she was being coerced into the decision or negotiated into it, but she turned when they did.

'Come.' Kalev didn't turn when he issued his orders. 'I need something that they have.'

The rope dangled uselessly into the middle of the void, anchored by the Irishman's dead weight so they would have to get across under their own steam.

Kalev had come prepared, with a pneumatic bolt and line launcher: compressed air fired a barbed climbing bolt towards the roof, and on the third attempt it hooked in a crack. He ripped off his suit jacket, scrunched it into a ball, and tossed it off the cliff; then he extended each arm, bent forward to stretch his hamstrings, and connected a carabineer to a length of climbing rope and started to pull himself upwards. 'Cover me. I'll secure the frontline. On my signal, you will follow.'

If the others were going to attack, they would do it now. But no shots came and four minutes later, he was just below the roof, aiming another bolt. It took twenty minutes to traverse the drop, hanging upside down with his knees interlocked and his hands pulling him forward.

He slid down to the far bank and took cover behind a large boulder a few paces in from the ledge. It still anchored the taut climbing rope, which he gave a playful twang.

Kalev sat down there, took off his headlamp, and clipped it to the rope, giving him a view of the space ahead without making his own head a too-obvious target. The tunnel was empty but full of shadows where a sniper could hide; he scanned his own gun back and forth, trying to cover them all. Satisfied that he was alone, he signalled for his partner to cross.

Kalev was getting edgy; this was not a trap, it was an escape, and that was worse. He turned back to measure his lieutenant's progress: he was taking too long. Staying in a crouch, Kalev scuttled forward to the next boulder; and then to next. He looked back: still only half way. *Paska,* they were getting away.

Kalev gave chase.

71

I s THIS how it felt to catch a break?

Matthys Rossouw had a smile plastered across his face, partly because of the thrill of racing a borrowed Royal Enfield Bullet through Hong Kong's streets, but mainly because he was en route to an appointment with a source. Wilsin was a fixer, a middleman. He linked undocumented imports to independent merchants or under-secured warehouses to interested parties, but a buyer was a buyer and for an outlandish finder's fee he'd agreed to tell Matthys about a man who'd arrived in the city a week before and was spending on a variety of illicit goods and services.

Matthys was counting on the timing not being a coincidence.

Hiko moved a piece of tandoor-baked fish around on his plate. Hin Ho Curry House was his favourite escape from the endless noodles and dumplings that constituted Cantonese fare, but today he wasn't hungry. He was too angry. More so now that Wilsin was late. By just four minutes so far, but if he was going to hit up Hiko for more money, the least he could do was be punctual. His men had been standing idle for fuck's sake, how exactly had they run up 'unexpected expenses'?

Hiko tapped the table for another minute before the bell above the door chimed. Wilsin walked in slowly, and wordlessly took a seat opposite Hiko. Then he sat with a tiny smile on his face, just waiting for Hiko to hand over the money.

Hiko took a deep breath, reminded himself that he had much more pressing matters to be concerned about, and pushed a thin envelope across the table. Wilsin prised it open an inch, nodded, and began to rise. He nodded over his shoulder. 'Our deal still stands, this is a separate issue.'

Hiko looked in the direction he was indicating. The bastard. The absolute bastard. He made a grab for the envelope still visible in Wilsin's pocket, but the little man was quicker.

A policeman had just pulled up on a motorbike. A beauty. Definitely not government-issue. And though the man was dressed in jeans and a red Tin Tin T-shirt, he may as well have had a flashing blue light on his head. Hiko could spot a policeman from a mile away. He turned and ran to the back of the restaurant, past the toilet, through a service door, and into a shabby courtyard that the sun lit with more lustre than it deserved. Stained walls guarded a patch of weed-cracked paving that seemed to be a halfway house for broken furniture not yet on the tip.

He scrambled up the pile of detritus and over the wall.

Matthys had a foot in the restaurant before he realised his mistake: this wasn't an information gathering exercise, it was now the take-down; though now, of course, it was too late and he'd already bungled it. He heard a gasp; a tray of plates crashing to the floor; angry shouts in Chinese; a door slamming shut; and then another burst of shouting.

All eyes in the room turned to him, then swung to the back of the restaurant, then swung back to him. Like a tennis match.

Matthys made brief eye contact with Wilsin and then sprinted through the narrow restaurant and out the back door, followed closely by the flustered owner. 'Hey, you must make him pay for this damage.'

Matthys scanned the courtyard. There were no hiding places. 'What's behind this wall?'

'Alley. You must make him pay, okay?'

Matthys clambered up a pile of broken chairs and looked over the wall, just in time to see St George turn into the main road.

The policeman vaulted the wall and gave chase.

72

HIKO FELT the landing in his knees but he didn't have time for self pity; unlike some parts of Hong Kong, Shau Kei Wan wasn't a warren of alleys so hiding wasn't an option, he'd have to run.

Hiko reached the main road and peered around the corner. The motorbike was still parked in front of the restaurant, but the policeman was gone. No doubt circling around behind him, then. That wasn't good.

At least he had a head start. And the lunchtime traffic would negate some of the benefit of the motorcycle.

Hiko ran on the road to avoid the even more clogged sidewalk, weaving between the cars parked on either side and those unwillingly stationary in the middle of it.

At the corner, Matthys caught sight of a fuzzy head bobbing and weaving between the cars. The bright orange T-shirt helped too. He turned left to fetch his bike.

Matthys pulled his phone out of his pocket as he ran; Gu was on speed dial. 'I've got him! Running down Shau Kei Wan Main Street East, towards the water.'

'*Do not engage him, Chief Inspector. I repeat—*'

Matthys kicked the engine to life, drowning out the end of Gu's instruction.

The roar of an engine told Hiko that he'd been spotted. He risked a look back. He had a lead approaching 200 metres, as well as the advantage of agility. The policeman had the advantage of outright speed.

Two hundred metres ahead of Hiko, the road split around an ancient fig tree, after which the traffic eased off. That raggedy tree became his short-term goal. He had to stretch his lead as much as he could, while he could.

Hiko stepped right, leapt over the low wall of a Taoist temple, sending the languid incense smoke into excited swirls, and buying himself a precious few paces. The bike was less than 100 metres away now, preceded by a bow wave of startled pedestrians. He leapt over the far wall, and cut back into the street.

The bike was now fifty metres behind him. Salvation appeared, in the form of a pedestrian subway.

'Stand down and observe! You have no authority to engage! We'll be there in less than ten minutes. I need you to see where he goes. That is all.'

Matthys kept the throttle fully open, weaving between cars and bumping on and off the road whenever he spotted a small gap.

St George was within reach.

Hiko grabbed the handrail and let his momentum spin him around and down a flight of stairs as the policeman skidded past, his hand rippled Hiko's jacket but failed to hold on.

Hiko bounded down the stairs four at a time. The subway passed underneath a major intersection and the police would either have to dismount and follow him on foot, or split up to cover all eight exits. Straight ahead lay the typhoon shelter and his fireboat.

The odds were back in his favour.

Matthys was off the bike before it had stopped, wincing at the sound of it crashing down and scraping against the tarmac, but not stopping to see the damage.

He bounded down the stairs in three long strides, hitting the ground too late to catch sight of his target, though the tiled walls still echoed with the drum of his footsteps. It was hard to be certain – especially with Gu still yelling instructions in his other ear – but Matthys felt like the sound was coming from dead ahead.

And then he saw him, twenty metres away, running up a ramp back to the surface.

Hiko looked over his shoulder. The policeman was close. But probably not close enough. Hiko burst out of the subway, turned right, and hurdled over the fence that bordered the waterfront park.

Matthys exited the ramp less than twenty seconds after St George, but it took him another twenty seconds to see where he'd gone, and by then the race was lost.

'Gu, he's somewhere in the Shau Kei Wan Typhoon Shelter. I'm observing.'

'We're two minutes away. Wait there.'

73

Like an upside-down caterpillar, Kalev's lieutenant moved by stretching his hands forward and pulling, stretching and pulling, stretching and . . . falling; the sting of a shot caught him off guard, and mocked his complacency as its retort echoed back and forth. Fortunately, he had been tied on. He bounced once and then dangled from his tether, his back now facing his enemy.

He ripped off his headlamp and dropped it, twisting to look over his shoulder, hoping to catch sight of the shooter in the plummeting beam, but everything below him was dark.

He patted his side. His hand came away sticky with blood, but not a lot of it; judging by the hole in his jacket, the bullet that nicked him had come from a small calibre weapon.

He was reaching for his own gun when a second shot flashed below. Another miss. Now he had a target. He fired twice; the recoil pushing him into a slow swing.

When Patrick fell, he was sure he was about to die. He didn't, but the rope that had caught him had also trapped him, suspending him somewhere between the roof above and the ground below.

There was nothing he could do, so he had waited. He had waited while Kalev crossed, he hated to, but his backup would have seen the gun flash and would have had little trouble taking Patrick out. He had waited for what seemed like forever, until finally an opportunity to halve the opposition forces presented itself.

And he had scorned it, since he could hear the man cursing.

Two shots, to the left and to the left again of where his target had once been. The first bullet twanged off the steel handle above Patrick's head and the second whistled past his ear before cracking the stone floor somewhere far below. Both men were blind, moving in intersecting orbits.

If this took too long and Kalev returned, any shot Patrick took would betray his location and seal his fate. So Patrick fired immediately, aiming a metre to the left of the last flash.

He missed and half his bullets were gone.

The Irishman must be moving, too. The latest shot had come from somewhere new. Or was he swinging more than he thought? It was hard to tell with no visible landmarks and dropping blood pressure. He fired again.

It was like the closing stages of a game of Battleship and he favoured the meticulous approach: shooting in a steady sequence, aiming straight down as Newton's Third Law pushed him backwards.

Bang. Miss. Bang. Miss. Bang. Miss. Bang. Hit!

Patrick heard the first shot pass ten metres to his left. One, one thousand. The second came five metres closer. Two, one thousand. The third shot passed close enough for him to smell it. Three, one thousand. Bang!

Kalev ignored the shooting for as long as he could. He didn't want to turn his back on the tunnel in case the others decided to head back his way, but being outflanked could happen from either side, so when the shooting persisted, he knew he had to retreat.

No one was waiting on the landing when he arrived. Kalev ran to the boulder that earlier had provided him shelter. He unsheathed a hunting knife, and with three quick slices, cut through the climbing rope that was still fastened to it.

He was sprinting back down in the tunnel before it had finished unspooling, his rear now secure.

74

S AM HELD up his hand, signalling the others to stop. 'This is where we make our stand.'

They had run further into the sharply turning tunnel system than they had wanted to, and all three were breathing heavily.

'Yeah, that'll—'

They spun towards a muffled sound: gunfire.

Brett ran six paces back towards it, turning only when she noticed she was alone. 'We need to go back!' Her shoulders slumped as she looked from Sam to Roman and back. 'God, you straight-up promised!'

Sam shook his head. 'It's a trick to flush us out. If we go back, we'll be running headlong into an ambush.'

'And if it's not? And if Patrick is in trouble?'

'Brett, I'm sorry. Even if it's not a ruse, it'll be over before we get there. Leaving him wasn't an easy decision, but it was the right one, and it is still the right one. There is nothing we can do.'

'Roman?' Brett took two steps back towards him. 'Roman? I should have expected another betrayal from Sam, but from you?'

'Sam's right, Brett. We can't change the outcome for Patrick and trying could get us killed. We're not well armed, we can't fight these guys head-to-head, we need this element of surprise.'

'Patrick's not a soldier. He's not even in this for the treasure. We have to help him. Can't you understand that? Sam? Roman?' Each man struggled to hold her stare.

Then the second volley of shots came and Brett started to sprint. 'Fuck you guys, I'm going to help him.'

She had rounded the first corner before the other two could react.

Sam placed a hand on Roman's shoulder. 'Let her go. She needs to let off some steam. She won't go far. And when she comes back, she'll be more pleasant to be around for it. The only way we can help her is by setting this trap.'

Kalev paused at the corner, stuck his head around it, then ran. He reached the next corner sweating more than the cool dry air required, paused, peeked, and ran again. His life was alternating between two-minute long gambles and the briefer moments of security offered by each corner. He peered around the next edge. No one was coming, so he ran again.

Halfway to the next corner, Kalev stopped: footsteps.

Brett skidded around the corner but dared not slow. While each shot had been a sign that Patrick was in mortal danger, it had also been a sign that he was probably still alive, and the slap of her shoes had been unpunctuated by shooting for too long now. She was getting worried. Surely she should have reached the crevasse by now. Surely?

And then the shooting started again; but much closer. Brett dived to the floor as it exploded around her, her momentum sliding her beyond the strike zone though she knew the unseen shooter would adjust. She rolled twice to her left as shots bit into the floor; then rolled back, praying that such a simple trick would work. It did. The wall to her left shed rough chips.

Brett jumped to her feet, spun and ran back the way she had come. She was too late. Patrick was dead. Because she'd asked him to help.

Kalev gave chase, furious with himself for shooting early. He had assumed it was all three of them and he hadn't taken the time to check. But it had been just her. Alone. It would have been such an easy kill. And now, like a week earlier, she was on the run, and once again he was chasing her, gaining a few metres before each turn, losing them again whenever he slowed to aim and shoot.

Kalev watched Brett disappear around the next corner a heartbeat before his bullets smacked into the wall; he was dealing in seconds, now. If he stopped trying to shoot her, he'd make up the ground in three or four turns, but did he have three or four turns to spare? The exit could be anywhere.

Kalev rounded the corner fifteen seconds after Brett and saw his best chance: she was in the longest section of tunnel he had seen so far, about a hundred metres ahead of him and a similar distance away from the next corner. Then she stopped and turned.

Although he admired her spirit, at this distance and in the dark, as an amateur, she had no chance. Kalev didn't even flinch. He raised his own gun as the first bullet struck the wall twenty metres in front of him, lined up his shot as the second bullet chipped the roof thirty metres behind him, exhaled as the third bullet bit into the floor ten metres to his right, inhaled as Brett turned to run, and exhaled as he squeezed the trigger.

Brett was fifty metres from safety and each of his shots had come progressively closer. Kalev exhaled and squeezed the trigger a fourth time.

Brett was thirty metres from the next corner when the bullet cut her down; her knee buckled first, then her momentum sent her into an awkward tumble across the slick floor. Her gun clattered into the shadows. Kalev ran towards her.

That her gun was lost didn't even register; it was all about survival now. Brett jacked herself to her knees. Summoning every memory of the energy her body once had, she popped herself up and limped forward. She had twenty metres to cover. Kalev must have been a similar distance behind her.

Her eardrums pounded with the close explosion of yet another shot; her arm was pierced and then stung by chips of stone as the bullet cut through her and crashed into the wall an inch away. There were five metres between her and the next corner.

A roar chased her as she limped around it, tugging at her jacket as she fell again.

Brett stood up and hopped forward. The tunnel here was littered with rubble where a section of the wall had collapsed; five metres away, a low mound of rocks and dirt spilled across her path.

Brett dropped over the mound as boots slid around the corner behind her.

Kalev fired twice.

A second gun fired a rapid burst over her ducked head. Kalev must have reloaded because an extended retort came back. Then a third gun joined the fray.

75

WHERE THE wall had collapsed, it had exposed a small recess, which Sam and Roman had worked to enlarge, scraping away loose rubble until it was large enough to conceal a man. Roman. Once he was inside, Sam had replaced the largest slabs of rock, rendering the hiding place virtually invisible, and then he had ferried rubble further down the tunnel to make the low barrier over which Brett had dropped, and then a second, higher barrier twenty metres deeper in. That's where he had waited.

The plan had been for Brett to wait there, too, and then when Kalev and his colleague rounded the corner, Sam would open fire. Ideally, they would then take cover behind the first barrier, allowing Roman to step out from his hiding place and shoot them in the back.

In the end, Brett had made her late and dramatic appearance, Sam had managed not to shoot her, and Roman had managed to shoot Kalev.

Brett's foul mood was more difficult to conquer. So Sam had left Roman to patch up her wounds, while he headed down the passage to find out what had become of Patrick and the missing gunman.

Brett took a deep glug of Roman's vodka and tested her duct tape bandages. He'd done a decent patch-up job. 'Where's Sam going?'

'To find Patrick.'

'To find Patrick's body, you mean?' Brett spat on the floor, dusted herself off, and marched deeper into the tunnel. She was going to find the treasure since she had already paid the admission price.

She would do it without Sam, though.

She would rather have done it without Roman, too, but he was following her like a stray dog and she didn't have the energy to chase him away.

After twenty minutes, the tunnel widened into a space the shape and size of a school hall, with seven doors cut into the far wall. They were identical, smooth and cast from solid bronze, each with a keyhole. She stopped at the last one and chose a key at random.

It fitted snugly. And when she turned the key, nothing happened. Brett removed that key and slid it into another door. It fitted, too. Just like earlier, every key fitted every door, though here every key did absolutely nothing. Brett took a step back and looked down the line. There was nothing to go on: there were no numerals or symbols on the floor, no decorations or furnishings in the space, nothing to fertilise the slightest guess. She turned to Roman. 'What do you suggest?'

'A shot of vodka?'

'Funny. But I'll take you up on that.' And she did. 'This has to be a code again, some sort of sequence: Visby, Tallinn, Riga, Gdansk, here?' she said, thumbing the keys in that order.

'Or maybe they're random and the code was passed down in secret.'

'Then we're screwed. I've changed my mind, though, the order of the clues is too easy, it's what we used to get us down here, which doesn't sit right.' Brett spun the keys around her finger and thought about the tools she had available. They'd always been enough before. She walked to the first door, flicked through the keys, slid one in and turned it. Nothing happened. She didn't expect it to. Brett moved to the second door, inserted a different key, and turned it. Nothing happened. She moved along the line, turning keys and possibly doing nothing, possibly solving the riddle.

In the order she'd used the keys, she'd watched the tiny etched dragon unfurl its wings in stop-motion steps and take off. The first etched dragon had been sitting on its perch, and now, as she turned the last key in the last door, the dragon etched on its shaft was in full flight.

With a loud click, the fourth door sprung open

Behind the door a stone bridge soared over another crevasse. The bridge was paved in small white bricks, ridged at intervals to provide more grip.

Brett ran up it, racing her nerves to the top, slowing down and then stopping when the vertigo overtook her. The bridge's shape was so graceful that it had belied her dizzying climb. Until then. Brett shone her torch down and groaned. She looked left and right and nearly started to cry, there was an identical bridge behind each door; the stones below her feet were now only as coherent as her guessed sequence.

The bridge wove in and out of her tunnelling vision as she battled an upsurge of nausea. She knew the bridge would collapse. She just hoped it would do it quickly and cut short her ordeal. Although she tried to turn around, her legs marched her forward.

76

BRETT WAS on solid ground. Behind her, Roman had started to cross; he was walking confidently, though she noticed he had waited for her to reach the other side before starting.

Together their twin beams lit a narrow room with an exceptionally high ceiling and no visible walls. There must have been walls, of course, but they couldn't see them; all they could see was a forest of hexagonal pillars receding in every direction.

The floor was paved with hexagonal tiles of black and white, but Brett's eyes were drawn upwards, to the rhythmic chaos above, to where the pillars, having risen unbending to the ceiling, broke free from the rigidity of their climb and wove themselves into a writhing tangle with no obvious start or end. She was seeking clarity up there when a protruding tile brought her physically and mentally back to earth.

It hadn't been a protruding tile that had tripped her, it had been a bronze ring embedded at the room's midpoint. It made the floor look like a giant cupboard door with the ring as its handle. Brett gripped it and pulled.

It didn't budge.

She chuckled, envisioning herself lifting the floor below her feet. Then she remembered the seriousness of the day's events.

She paused to gather her strength and tugged it again. It still didn't move. So she twisted the handle. And it turned easily, with a gentle rustle.

Brett and Roman spun around, braced for attack, but all they saw was the same empty room. Brett turned the ring again. The sound was like a thousand twirling ball gowns, and fleeting; and once again their torches failed to find its source among the pillars.

'Do it again.'

While Brett turned the ring, Roman scanned the shadows.

'Brett, it's incredible.'

She looked where he was looking, and saw nothing. 'What is it?'

'They moved.' Roman's eyes were wide.

'Who did?'

'The pillars. Turn it again and watch.'

Brett turned the ring and watched the pillars do nothing until, as the ring completed its full rotation, they spun swiftly and in unison. The room looked the same afterwards, yet also somehow different. There was still a forest of hexagonal bamboo, but the angles had shifted: narrow paths were now open where none had existed before, while some of those that previously existed had now been closed.

Was that how it worked?

Brett turned the ring again, and again: they watched as the changing angles promised paths through the stone forest without ever delivering one.

77

SAM HEARD singing, very soft, very bad singing. He snorted. 'God, stop that before I shoot you.'

Sam holstered his gun and ran forward to give Patrick a hand. He looked quite well actually, his hair was plastered flat with sweat, his hands red and raw, and the climbing rope coiled over his shoulder weighed him down, but given the ordeal he'd just been through it was remarkable that he was walking at all.

Patrick's face lit up in a broad grin when he saw Sam. 'You should see the other guy,' Patrick said, anticipating the obvious question. 'It got close at the end but I got lucky, poor lad. Not his day and all that.'

'How are you, really?'

'Really? Knackered. I had to climb up that rope like the tax man was chasing me, in case Kalev came back. Which he did – and he cut the rope, the fecker – but fortunately I had reached the roof by then and was rifling through his colleague's pockets. He didn't see me. Fortunately again, I must add. And they say good things come in threes, don't they? Since you're here to greet me personally, can I assume that I don't have to worry about Kalev anymore?'

'Yeah, he's been dealt with. Our only threat now is Brett, who has very real plans to do to me what he couldn't, I fear.'

'Ha, ha. Well, I'll try to put in a good word.'

Roman offered Patrick a drink, which he turned down, though he did indulge in Brett's hugs and curses. 'Patrick, I'm so sorry. I wanted to go back, but they . . . I thought . . . I thought he'd killed you and I couldn't face that.'

'Don't worry, you couldn't have done anything. And I had it all under control.'

'Oh, Patrick . . . I'm so glad you did. And I need your help.'

'Right, put him straight to work, then.' Patrick dodged Brett's playful punch.

'I need your help with some geometry. You deal with that every day, don't you? Being an "architect" and all that,' Brett said, using air quotes.

A minute later, they all watched the pillars spin as Brett turned the bronze ring.

'So, what do you make of it?' Brett asked. 'There must be a way to clear a path all the way through.'

'Maybe it's as basic as having to turn it a certain number of times,' Sam said.

Brett turned the ring again in a huff. 'We've all had a tough day, but you'll need to do better than that if you want me to take you seriously.'

'I wonder why that one doesn't turn,' Patrick said, after a minute of watching.

Brett turned the ring again. Patrick was right, one row back, there was a single pillar that never spun. Brett turned the ring again, until a narrow gap opened to it.

Carved into the stationary pillar's base was a dragon with its wings extended, like one of the amber globes. They were right. 'Okay, so what do we do now?' Brett asked Patrick.

Patrick stared at the pillar. Tapped it. 'Well, how do the others turn?' he asked.

'That's the sort of architectural insight I was hoping to get out of you.'

'Okay. Okay. Well, there are a few options.' Patrick looked at his audience, suddenly the picture of a professor. 'The simplest design would have the pillars turning on something, something like a ball bearing. Hopefully a lot like a ball bearing, because we've got a bunch of amber ones.' He rattled the duffle bag. 'Can we lift the pillar?'

The pillar was about as wide as a man's embrace; they knew this because Roman had just wrapped his arms around it. Roman dropped onto his haunches, grunted, and then jerked himself upwards. To the surprise of everyone – himself included – the pillar lifted easily, rising an inch before he dropped it back, gripping his shoulder.

Sam rushed to the other side of the pillar and grabbed it too. Roman counted down from three and together they raised the pillar upwards and held it in place as Patrick rolled an amber globe in underneath. It settled with a clink.

Roman locked eyes with Brett. She shrugged.

'Come on, this thing is heavy and some of us have been shot today; and again two days before that, if we're counting.'

'Okay, okay, put it down, you big drama queen.'

Roman and Sam eased the pillar down and watched it for longer than there was any logical reason too. The amber didn't break, but nothing else happened, either.

'Try turning the ring now,' Patrick said, dusting his hands on his pants though he hadn't done any of the heavy lifting.

They watched as Brett turned the bronze ring. The pillars followed, all of them, coming to rest in a new alignment that opened the path by another five metres.

'We have more dragons, of course.' Brett said, once it was clear that nothing else was going to happen. 'So there must be more stationary pillars, mustn't there?'

Everyone watched closely and Brett continued to turn the ring, until a second immobile pillar, diagonally back and to the right of the first one, was spotted.

The path opened up progressively slower from there. The pillars were so close together that it wasn't safe to wait among them between each turn, so they had to find a new stationery pillar, retreat, spin the ring, return to the spot, and then fan out as best they could, searching for the next one marked with a tiny engraved dragon.

'Over here.' They were fifty metres into the stone jungle when Sam spotted the final pillar. At least they hoped it was the final one because afterwards, they'd be out of globes, and ideas.

Brett turned the ring one last time. She paused for a second, looked at the others, and then rushed down the path, intent on getting there first. The three men followed a step behind. They knew the route well by now, even as it jagged right and left, though at the last pillar they had to stop again, just for a moment, to search for their final destination.

It had to be there.

And it was. Patrick waved his torchbeam to grab their attention: to their left, visible through a new gap in the pillars, was a path of cobblestones, the mortar that bound them glinted under his light. It really was paved with gold. Sort of.

Patrick stepped back and let Brett go first. She skipped down the path, stopping at an arched doorway to absorb the scene in front of her.

They had found the treasure. Her reflected torch beam formed unpredictable and unstable combinations. Light danced on the walls and ceiling in warm and liquid hues, it spun and collided and scattered like giddy children on a sugar high. After so many architectural fantasies, the treasure chamber was very plain: another domesticated cave, whittled into the sort of proportions you might get if drew a hexagon with your left hand; assuming you were obsessed with gold, of course, because the space was soaked in it.

Gold undulated over every surface and dripped down the walls like Christmas tinsel.

Brett dived in.

78

WITH THE bottleneck uncorked, Patrick, Roman, and Sam rushed in, slowing as they absorbed the spectacle.

Brett picked up a gold nugget and squeezed it in her palm, as she turned full circle in the room's centre. She dropped the nugget and walked deeper. 'Just look at this place. I never. . . .' She shook her head and picked up an emerald the size of an apple; just one of a fruit salad of giant jewels that decorated her footprints. 'I mean, just look at this place.'

The emerald was inexpertly cut and far from flawless, but it was the most spectacular green she had ever seen. She put it down.

Next to it lay a coil of necklaces, freed from the confines of a decayed hemp bag. Each bead on the one she picked up was a smooth gold oblong, spotted with tiny black stones and threaded by a thin gold string.

Floating on the tide of gold nuggets was a scattered flotsam of larger objects: decorative masks, ceremonial weapons, and chunky jewels, all of which glittered under the scanning torches as the party waded across the room.

She had found the *Drachen*. And now she had found its treasure. There was so much to take in. So much to take, actually. Roman said he could find a buyer that would pay a good price for any of the pieces. Though as a team they'd agreed on a compromise, a moral cop-out. They'd help themselves to what they felt was an appropriate finder's fee, and then make an anonymous call to alert the authorities, leaving anything too heavy pull out and enough of the lower value items to make it look like an undisturbed find. And even then, except perhaps for Roman, none of them were very interested in monetising their find.

A few metres away, Sam was standing, quietly smiling, while Roman and Patrick chased each other with heavy pockets, engaged in a playful gold ball fight.

Brett waded towards a unique item: three two-metre-long ivory tusks bound together to form a pedestal that stood out starkly against the gold background. On top sat a squat wooden sculpture. Brett gave the pedestal a shake. It was rock solid. The loose treasure was deeper there, nuggets were almost up to her knees as she circled it.

The tusks were interesting too. The roll of laughter and the clatter of intentionally misdirected nuggets faded as she took in the detail.

The ivory was polished to a high sheen, highlighting the thin spiral of symbols that curled around each tusk from base to summit. They weren't Egyptian hieroglyphics, nor were they the pictographs that had decorated the bronze disks and the coded stories; in fact, they looked more like motifs from a Louis Vuitton bag than any form of writing Brett had ever seen. She counted twenty-four different symbols, all simple geometric shapes and all vertically symmetrical, ranging from the simple to the intricate.

Brett gave it another shake. Still no movement. So they would be staying there. She took out her phone and videoed the lines of symbols.

Then she started throwing nuggets at the sculpture. Toppling it after a dozen attempts.

She doubted it was worth the effort. Slimy to the touch and sharp with the vinegar odour of decay, it was smaller than a shoebox, amateurishly carved with some of the same symbols that decorated the tusks, and closed tight by a band of silver that had been poured into its seams. It was light. And when Brett shook it, silent.

Sam had woken from his lull and was clearing a space near the door. Patrick and Roman had stopped their games and were now picking prime items from the buffet. She slipped the box into the nearest bag without really knowing why, and wandered across to join the others. 'Any thoughts on what we do next?'

'We're prepping the first load. Once we've packed these bags we can take them out, then we'll bring in some forklifts to haul out the bigger stuff.'

'Except we don't have a way out, do we? The bridge isn't there anymore and I don't fancy swinging across that crevasse carrying a ton of gold.'

Sam stopped working and pinched the bridge of his nose as he looked back towards the chamber's entrance. 'You're right. So we need a back door. Any ideas?'

'I'll look around while you finish up here.'

'Be my guest.' Sam turned back to the series of village scenes that he'd been shuffling through: they looked like Russian icons, except that they were made from solid gold rather than wood. He put them aside and picked up a small wooden box, sliding it open to reveal a ring, its band marked with a branching pattern and topped by a translucent teal stone.

He slipped that into his pocket as a gift for his wife, then picked up a small bowl studded with so many diamonds that it looked like leaded glass. Priceless. He put it into the duffle bag and turned his attention to a gold dagger encrusted with garnets. Nice, but also just very valuable. He put it aside. He could afford to be that picky.

Once Brett found the way out – because with this much motivation she surely would – they had a simple plan: Brett would walk back into Dötlingen rent a van while the men continued to lift out the best pieces; then, when Brett returned, they'd start running loads to a warehouse in Bremen that Patrick would arrange for them; they'd do as many loads as they could before nightfall; and then they'd have a drink.

Shadowed recesses hinted at doorways, but none held up to closer examination. Everywhere Brett looked, the rock walls were solid and unbreached.

She moved back towards the middle of the room, scanning the ceiling now, too, all the while dreading the possibility that the exit would be up there.

'Brett, have you ever seen anything like this?' Patrick waved a chalice cut from garnet; backlit like that, it was flaming red.

As Brett stepped towards Patrick, her foot sent a diamond-encrusted sceptre skittering across the floor, which was taking on an air of familiarity as black and white hexagonal tiles began to appear in the patches where the gold had been cleared away.

Brett tilted her head. Were their sides straight? She forgot about the chalice and dropped to a knee. She scraped the nuggets away. No, no they weren't. The tiles were subtly slanted, a distortion that became more obvious as Brett hopped from cleared patch to cleared patch, now racing towards the chamber's midpoint.

The design was incredible, made to look like the whole floor was being dragged down a whirlpool. And Brett wanted to see where it culminated. She studied the pattern, estimated the location of its focus, and took four big steps forward.

She pushed the nuggets away until she could see the floor. Then she moved a step to the left and started again. She stood up, shrugged, and stamped her foot.

The room rattled. Then a shaft of light flashed in, followed by a confetti of falling stones and dirt.

A bronze dragon the size of her open palm had been embedded at the tiles' focal point. She had guessed it was a lock release and she had been right. But Brett cursed: the thin crack of sunlight outlined an opening in the roof, and illuminated a perilous trail of handholds chipped into the wall, visible now that they were lit from above. They would be climbing out, after all. 'Is everyone all right?' she asked.

'Yeah, thanks for the warning and all that.' Sam was brushing dust from his shoulders. Brett stopped behind the others and stared up, even though she knew she shouldn't.

'Let's assume that's our way out, then,' Sam said. 'We'll need to come back, of course, but I think we're ready to take out some gold. Anyone else fancy a breath of fresh air?'

'I'm in.' Patrick zipped the last bag closed and stood. Sam and Roman's backpacks, the duffle bag, and the five ripstop nylon bags they'd brought along were stuffed with their equipment and the choicest artefacts; and they'd just scraped the pile. The nuggets were the easiest to turn into cash, of course, but they were only worth their literal weight in gold and that was a literal weight they'd have to lug out of there, so they'd concentrated on the items with higher value-to-weight ratios. None among them was an expert, but they'd been able to pick out some clear masterpieces.

Patrick tested the weight of two bags, lifted one onto his back and passed the other to Brett. Then he swung another over his free shoulder.

79

THE CLIMBING ropes, carabineers, bolts, and quick draws had all been laid out in groups. Patrick was already strapped into a climbing harness and holding a similar one towards Brett, softening the blow with a smile. Brett appreciated the effort, but still had to suppress panic as she stepped into it.

As it turned out, the length of rope that Patrick had salvaged would be long enough to reach the roof, so Sam would lead the climb, screwing anchoring bolts into the few viable cracks he passed so the others could follow with the aid of a safety line.

Sam reached the roof, paused to recapture his breath, then shoved the stone slab fully open.

Below him he heard Brett groan. 'I can't stand around here waiting. It will kill me. I need to go next.'

Patrick worked quickly, looping the rope through her harness and checking her connections before she lost her nerve. He tugged the rope and shouted up to Sam, 'She's on!'

'Wait.' Brett wriggled in the harness.

'You'll be fine, you're tied in and perfectly safe.'

'What do I do if I start to fall?'

'The rope loops through an anchor at the top so you're completely safe; I've got the other end and won't let you fall. You won't even need to climb, we'll pull you up.'

'Thanks but . . . I know it's stupid, but I need to feel like I'm in control.'

'It's not stupid. Okay, I'm operating the main brake but this here, in your harness, is a backup. It operates like a car seatbelt; if you fall more than a metre, it'll jam the rope and stop you.'

'And leave me hanging? Up there?'

'No, not at all. All you need to do is hold the rope to the side like this and you'll start to slowly descend. Let it go again and you'll stop. It's as easy as that.'

'Are you sure?'

Patrick started pulling the rope by way of reply, dragging her up the rock face before she could get worked up again.

Brett, for her part, closed her eyes and bounced upwards, trying to believe she was floating in a pool, until she felt Sam grip her shoulder straps. With a grunt, he pulled her out and deposited her on the grass.

Brett kept her safety harness on and scrambled a metre further away, before shouting down, 'I'm okay!'

Sam leaned into the hole and relieved Roman of the bags slung over his shoulders and helped him out.

Roman stood, stretched, and took in a magnificent breath, and then wrapped Sam in a bear hug; together the two friends walked towards Patrick, already discussing how they would spend their share of the spoils.

They had emerged from a low open-faced granite lean-to, topped by a flat granite slab; part of a larger formation of placed boulders: a stone Viking ship, set in a clearing on a small peninsula where the stream horseshoed on itself.

80

DÖTLINGEN WAS several miles away, and given the sun-faded informational plaque and overgrown tracks between the stones, few tourists made that trek.

On the plus side, it meant that they were unlikely to be noticed, hauling bags full of ancient gold from out the ground. On the negative side, it meant Brett had to leave the treasure in the others' hands for a few hours while she fetched the rental van.

It had always been the plan, but she still looked over her shoulder every minute as she walked away, until the men were lost from view. Ten minutes later, she crossed a simple wooden bridge and the smoking chimneys of the village came into view.

After thirty minutes spent rigging ropes, the three men were back in the chamber. The falling boulders had landed in formation and now looked like outcrops in a sea of gold.

The late afternoon sun brushed the chamber in honeyed light and revealed new details in the treasure and the walls that contained it.

Sam stood silently, turning a mask in his hands: it was carved from ebony, a ruby the size of a golf ball glowed in each eye socket, and the hair was spun gold wire. He put it aside and picked up a heavy gold bowl.

Even at second sight the treasure was a breathtaking in its scope and beauty. He just wished he didn't feel so hollow. Or was it natural to fall into a funk at the end of a quest? The gold should have helped more, there was so much of it after all. But would his grandfather be happy? Proud? Would he care? That's actually what it boiled down to: his grandfather never needed proof. But Sam did. Why had he not tried harder to find the proof?

His grandfather's obsession with the book had made him, if not an object of ridicule, then at least a character too quirky for official commendation after the war. This had all been for him and it would be fitting for Sam to use the find to resurrect his legacy. Or was it too late for that?

Didn't his grandfather deserve more than a contrite, 'You were right'?

Sam stood up and carried the mask to the waiting pallets. It would take Brett a couple of hours to get back with the van and he hoped to have the next load ready by then. If they worked quickly, they would be able to do three trips before it got dark.

They also worked quickly because Kalev's mysterious funder must have known, at least roughly, where he was heading; and when Kalev failed to check in, he'd surely send backup. With the big holes in the ground surrounded by piles of gold, it wouldn't be hard to find and overrun them.

'A round of beers?' Patrick was already signalling to the waiter. 'I think our day calls for a toast.'

They were back at their hotel, showered, changed, and after sweet-talking their host into re-opening the kitchen, sitting on the veranda awaiting a hearty dinner. Somewhere behind them the bell tolled in St Firmin's Church. Ten o'clock, just sixteen hours since they had first broken open the church's floor.

'Sure, but you can't toast with beer, not where I come from.' Roman grabbed the waiter when he arrived. 'A bottle of vodka, please. The best you've got, I'm treating my friends.' Turning back to the others, he smiled. 'Do you think this is a "euros-only" sort of a place, or do you think they'll accept old money as payment?' He rolled a gold coin across the table.

'I'm sure they'll be accommodating.' Brett laughed and pulled three garnet cups from under the table. 'And I say we drink it out of these.'

'To Brett!' they all cheered.

'And to treasure.'

'Treasure!'

81

NONE OF the mistakes Matthys had made mattered now:
St George had given them the run-around, true, but
now they had him cornered. Finally. The warrant had taken
two hours to secure, and all the while St George had been holed
up in a decommissioned fireboat floating a teasing thirty
metres offshore.

Matthys could still salvage this operation. Actually, Gu
could still salvage it for Matthys, he was leading a team closer
on land, coordinating his approach with the three high-speed
Marine Police boats that blockaded the typhoon shelter.

Gu directed his team with subtle hand gestures, placing
them along the promenade, blocking every possible land escape
route.

Matthys watched the action from well back, accompanied
by a police liaison officer, clearly there to make sure he behaved.

Matthys checked his watch: one minute to go. He liked
watches, he collected them, mechanical watches, interesting
ones, cheap ones – he was only a policeman, after all. He'd
picked up this one that week: hand assembled in Hong Kong
by the Perpetual Watch Company, its black dial and elegant
accents suited a gentleman, he thought, and for the equivalent

of one hundred euros, it packed in a lot of character. A bargain if it survived the day.

Everything was in place.

Things were falling apart. To the winner go the spoils. The others had found the chamber – and stripped it. By the time his team got there, there was very little gold left. And not a single viable mould sample. Hiko would have to write off this operation. Start afresh.

He activated a timer, then walked over to the old stereo, turned up the music and picked up the open bottle of Van Ryn's.

If he was going to go down, it would be with good music in his ears and the warmth of the world's best brandy on his lips. Maybe he was his father's son. That's *if* he was going to go down . . . he still had one card left to play. Hiko pulled out his phone and made a final call.

It was answered after two rings. 'Eliminate the target.'

His mother would still meet her doom. If not with the mould, then with something else. As long as he was free, he'd make sure that came to pass. And as long as that snake Wilsin was true to his final promise.

He slumped back and drank slowly, savouring the brandy and enjoying the music for one peaceful minute. Then he rose and walked to the window, opened it, and tossed his phone into the harbour. The police were close. He could see them spread across the promenade and park. At least a dozen of them, advancing carefully. Glass shattered somewhere to his left. A shot gonged against the hull near the waterline. Hiko stepped away from the window as more shots followed. Left, right, above, and below.

Hiko scrambled through a mist of shattered glass as his small world entropied.

Gu held his hand up, and his team stopped in unison. A shadow had moved behind a window on the fireboat's wheelhouse. They had their man. Matthys pumped his fist in silent celebration.

And then the shots came.

The team scrambled for cover. Even the boats spun away from the melee, seeking shelter behind the harbour wall. The shadow was gone, but the shooting hadn't stopped. It wasn't coming from the fireboat.

Gu rolled behind a bench, drew his gun, and scanned the promenade: two teenagers, standing like movie gangbangers with a gun held sideways in each hand, were shooting at the fireboat, their guns jerking in their grips, their wayward shots rattling the boat and holing its windows. *What on earth?*

'Drop your weapons,' Gu stood and bellowed at the gunmen. They just spun around and started shooting at him, instead.

The promenade exploded into a battlefield as his colleagues returned fire from all sides.

Bullets ripped through foliage and ricocheted off swings, walls, and lamp posts. Gu was losing control of the situation.

One of the young gunmen made a break, firing over his shoulder as he sprinted towards the low harbour wall; his companion, apparently having seen rather too many Triad movies, chose to counter-attack: with both guns spitting, he ran straight at Gu.

Gu pivoted and shot from the hip as bullets crashed around him. His first shot went wide, but the second one felled the youth mid-stride, taking him out of the picture. Gu swung back towards the first gunmen but the young man had already made it to cover behind a concrete mooring bollard.

Gu ducked back down to reload, taking the opportunity to check on his team: they had regained their composure and were moving forward in a defensive formation, covering each other and closing in on the last gunman, who was resisting his inevitable capture with a sprawl of panicked shots.

Gu yelled for calm.

Hiko opened the cabin door and skidded across the damp deck. The fighting was now concentrated on the shore, though the odd bullet still pinged off the fireboat's frame as he ran.

He slid behind a raised air vent and waited there, catching his breath. Then in three strides, he was across the deck and diving over the side.

The water was thick with filth and offered a physical resistance as he broke through its surface, sending up a foam of cardboard, polystyrene, and boat oil.

82

MATTHYS WAS part of the first team to board the fireboat, and he sat with the crime scene team that came later to search it.

They found not a single personal item, neither on deck nor below. Nothing. The man had lived up to his legend. He was a phantom.

Only the cabin showed any sign of use, though that, too, was a forensic desert: a small hi-fi serenaded pockmarked furniture and a smouldering computer, while a torn cable sparked in one corner. The trash in the water around the fireboat had been equally unhelpful. The Marine Police had arrived within five minutes of the first shots being fired and had blockaded the typhoon shelter's exit. They had also searched every boat in the shelter or passing nearby. Nothing.

The gunmen they had arrested had been useless as witnesses: two wannabe street thugs; one had broken into tears the moment the cuffs went on and the other one was still in a hospital bed, talking freely but pointlessly. He knew nothing. They had been watching the fireboat for a week, awaiting a signal to kill its occupant; that signal had been received moments before Matthys' team pounced, leading to the fracas. The men's phones had been checked and they had indeed received a text, from a phone that was now off and untraceable, of course.

The Hong Kong police removed the last of the crime scene tape and officially gave up the manhunt. St George was gone. Any career credits Matthys had built up in the hunt were gone, too. And maybe one day that would bother him. Maybe even one day soon. But for now, he was content to watch the returning fisherman drop their hand lines into the dark water.

Made in the USA
Middletown, DE
22 February 2016